KISS ME AGAIN

SECOND CHANCES

JESSA JAMES

GET A FREE BOOK!

Join my mailing list to be the first to know of new releases, free books, special prices and other author giveaways.

http://freehotcontemporary.com

Kiss Me Again: Copyright © 2020 by Jessa James

All Rights Reserved. No part of this book may be reproduced or transmitted in any form or by any means, electrical, digital or mechanical including but not limited to photocopying, recording, scanning or by any type of data storage and retrieval system without express, written permission from the author.

Published by Jessa James
James, Jessa
Kiss Me Again

Cover design copyright 2020 by Jessa James, Author
Images/Photo Credit: Deposit Photos: mjth

Publisher's Note:
This book was written for an adult audience. The book may contain explicit sexual content. Sexual activities included in this book are strictly fantasies intended for adults and any activities or risks taken by fictional characters within the story are neither endorsed nor encouraged by the author or publisher.

This book has been previously published.

1

COLE

"You have to be kidding me. Jacob, are you seriously going to let Callie set up a dating app? Well, my friend, there goes your reputation for being a serious mover and shaker in the tech world!"

I couldn't help but laugh at poor Jake's desperate attempts to get Callie's attention. He really would let her have whatever she wanted, the poor fool. I couldn't deny that she was smart too and her hunches were usually spot on, but this idea seemed a step too far in my humble opinion. But Callie was also the only woman I have ever met who could out-code me, and even had the temerity to beat me at chess – every single time. Well, of course, there had also been one other person who'd been able to do that, but she was no longer in my life. And yet, even five years later, my one true love Lucy still managed to infiltrate my thoughts at the most random times.

I shook my head and tried to force myself to pay attention to the conversation at hand. Maybe Callie had a different angle on the new dating app, one that hadn't already been done to death. Jacob grinned at me sheepishly and shrugged.

"Ha, ha, Cole!" Callie said sarcastically as she brought a pitcher of beer and three shots of tequila back from the bar. "You boys ready to celebrate? This is going to be the best idea we've ever put into production!"

We'd all met at UCLA, on the very first meeting of the year of the Tech Society. We had bunched around a table, admiring the new gadgets we had all been excited to receive to start college in true nerd style. We discussed every little improvement and flaw as if the world would end if they weren't put right – and then Callie walked in.

Standing six feet tall, she was a vision of leggy, blonde-haired, blue-eyed perfection. Naturally we all assumed she was in the wrong room. Turned out she was just as bright and obsessed as we all were, and more so than many. Callie truly did deserve the term 'wiz' – everything she did was fast: she thought fast, she drank faster, and she could solve virtually any math puzzle in moments.

And though there was no doubting that Callie was attractive, my heart belonged to another. The three of us settled into a comfortable friendship that lasted throughout college and beyond.

Callie knocked back her tequila shot and gestured to us to do the same. The fiery liquid burned its way down my throat and I made a face of pure displeasure. It had never been my drink; I was more of a bourbon guy really. I shook my head and regained my composure.

I must have still looked skeptical because I couldn't see it myself. Sure, dating sites and apps seemed to be big business, but surely there were already a hundred all doing exactly the same thing? I mean how many did the world truly need?

"Seriously guys, the market seems flooded, I know. But, I've done the research. Every site has a different angle – matching by compatibility; matching on hobbies; matching on lifestyle; even matching on pets. But none of them give you a chance to check out the entire pool of people out there looking for 'The One'. I mean, when you meet someone in a bar, you don't check out whether you have stuff in common. You go on attractiveness, do they make you laugh, does being around them make you go tingly – you know, all that kind of stuff."

I could kind of see her point. I have never waited to find out if a girl had something in common with me to go and ask her on a date. That's what first dates are for after all. There does need to be some kind of initial gut reaction that draws you in.

"I think I get it, but the point of internet dating is to cut out the selection process, to speed it all up for yourself, to be matched with someone you are likely to get along with right?" I asked, beginning to get genuinely curious but still prepared to play devil's advocate for the moment.

"For some people yes, time is of the essence – professionals and the like, but college kids have all the time in the world. Think about how Facebook started. It was a way to check out people on campus," Callie continued.

Jake nodded. "And let's face it, so many of us just don't have the guts to admit to the object of our desires how we feel."

I almost choked on my beer as he said so; his puppy-dog eyes were trained on the face of the woman who held his heart. If it hadn't been so hideously close to home I would have laughed out loud.

"Exactly. Look at us, bunch of geeks that we are. Not one of us has ever had the guts to go up to anyone and ask them out, yet we aren't even the worst of our kind. Cole Kent here is even kind of hot!" Callie joked.

"I've asked girls out on dates, occasionally... sometimes. I'm just not looking for anybody right now. You two could try a little harder, though. Neither of you is cursed with horn-rimmed glasses or nervous tics," I teased back.

"We know," Callie said as she rolled her eyes, "you fell in love at, like, age five and never fell out again..."

I sighed and tried to avoid her gaze, wanting her to change the subject.

"At some point you're going to have to accept that the constant weekend trips all around the country are not going to bring her back and just move on. When you do, my friend, you are going to be so glad that there will be an app that will help you find the perfect girl for you!"

I knew deep down Callie wasn't being harsh, and that she was probably right, but it still stung to hear it. I knew I couldn't let go, not yet at least. I'd spent the last five years searching everywhere, often with my stepfather Tom, for my stepsister Lucy. And it seemed like every time we went out I got neck-ache from the constant straining to see if her face was somewhere in the crowd.

She had been my best friend for as long as I could remember, and our mothers had been best friends too since high school. We'd grown up with each other;

morning coffee for our moms turned into play dates for us and as we got older we became inseparable.

But our friendship came under strain as disaster after disaster hit us like unrelenting waves. As if our teenage years weren't bad enough, we had to deal with death, betrayal and then a marriage we just hadn't seen coming.

Lucy left home not long after when my mom and her dad announced that they were getting married. My dad left my mom when I was just a kid. We hadn't heard from him in years. We were better off without him, but it had been so tough when he left. Lucy had been there for me through everything, let me cry on her shoulder, kept me in school, and made sure I didn't let my grades slip. I'd tried to do the same for her when her mother got cancer. It was the toughest time of all our lives; we were all so close, did everything together, and shared so much love between our two little families. Joanna, Lucy's mom, had made my mom and Tom promise to keep the families together. They had tried to do what she had wanted, and it had cost them Lucy, who just couldn't accept that her dad had moved on so quickly, or that my mom could betray her best friend.

I tried so hard to reason with her, but that made me as guilty as them in her eyes. She didn't want to hear anything that she didn't agree with. And then she was gone, and I lost the best friend and most wonderful girl in the world. Considering the miles Tom and I had covered between us and the college campuses we had visited, I had to agree with Callie. I probably wouldn't find her again.

And even if I did there was still the fact she was my stepsister to get past. Sure, we weren't related by blood or anything, but way too many people would think it was wrong, and she probably would too. Maybe she never felt the same about me anyway. I always dreamed our friendship could become more, but something always seemed to get in the way.

"Earth to Cole? Anyone home? Sorry honey, I didn't mean to sound so cruel," Callie touched a slender hand to my arm, her nails as always perfectly manicured in a bright scarlet shade that shone and twinkled in the light. This little touch always amused me, as she never wore any other makeup, just her trademark talons that clicked loudly as she typed at record speed.

"No, you're right. I need to move on. But what have you brought me here for? You guys don't normally bring me in on all the goings-on at Glitch. Clearly you don't want my advice on whether I think this is a good idea or not."

A cheesy grin spread all over Jake's moon-shaped face. "Well, we were wondering if you had time to do the coding for the app? I am snowed under with the updates to all the games, Callie is up to her ears with those odd girly recipe games and coupon apps and things she deals with," Jake admitted.

They often threw me the odd coding job when they were snowed under. I had to admit I was grateful. They paid me well and it meant I had managed to make it through college and a year into law school without any student loans to pay off. Considering our family didn't have much money to spare it had been a real godsend.

"Way to diminish some of the most successful apps we have on the books Jake," Callie tried to look huffy, but only succeeded in grinning as idiotically as Jake.

They waited for my answer, both staring at me intently. Obviously, they were truly excited, and that usually bode well for them and their bank accounts. Their first project together, a search app for on-campus societies at UCLA, had been so popular that every university had requested they do one for them. They had dropped out, and never looked back – except to make sure I wasn't floundering without them.

I considered the offer, trying to figure out if I could work it into my upcoming busy schedule. Callie's nails tapped impatiently upon the table.

"Well, I do have my internship starting at the DA's office in a few weeks, but I could probably have the bulk of it done for you by then, depending on how complex you need it," I said and smiled.

They simultaneously breathed a sigh of relief – they had both been holding their breath for my response. They raised their beer glasses for a toast.

"To 'Wooed and Won' – it's going to make us all filthy rich!" Callie cried happily. "Cheers!" We clinked the glasses loudly and drank deeply. Jake indicated to the bartender to bring another round of shots and it wasn't long before we were all drunk as skunks.

"Hey Jake, you entering the eating contest?" the bartender asked as he brought another pitcher of beer to the table.

"Eating contest? Show me where and when!" Jake exclaimed enthusiastically, rising from his chair and almost falling straight back down. He just about managed to maintain his composure as we giggled and he headed off toward the stage.

"Oh poor baby, he thinks it's going to be an all-you-can-eat thing," Callie said, concern in her tinkling, mocking girly voice. "He will never manage to eat half the stuff on this list." She was reading the flyer the bartender had left. I took it from her.

"You underestimate him Callie. I've seen him devour things that have made better men cry. There's nothing on here he can't get down. He'll be fine."

Callie looked at me, and I could swear I saw her eyes narrow. One of her eyebrows arched up and a mischievous glint appeared in her eyes. That couldn't be a good, I thought.

"Want to bet on it Kent?"

"Oh, really now?"

"Come on, put your money where Jake's mouth is," she chuckled.

"Why not, a nice friendly bet? Jake will not let me down when it comes to food."

"Let's choose some stakes shall we? If you win, what do you want from me?"

"That you do your impression of Tina Turner, on this table, tonight, in front of everyone," I said, thinking of the one thing that would freak her out the most. She gulped nervously but rallied pretty quickly.

"Okay, I want you to be the first person to sign up to the app once the site is up and running, and I want you to date at least one girl from the site a week for a whole month."

Now it was my turn to gulp. That was a pretty big stake.

"That's not very fair..." I grumbled. "If I win you only have to be embarrassed for a max of five minutes, but if I lose I'll have four night's worth of torture to contend with!"

"Chicken?" she asked as she poked her tongue out. "Hey, think of it as you'd be doing us a favor. The girls who sign up will be ecstatic to get a date with you Cole. The feedback from them could be amazing for us. And you never know, you might even find the woman of your adult dreams, not just your childhood ones."

"Fine! Sure, why not." I crossed my fingers under the table and prayed I would not regret it.

2

LUCY

"You did what?!" I yelled as Alison just grinned at me inanely. "How could you do something so stupid? I am not lonely. I do not need you to try and fix me up with your hairdresser's sister's cousin. And I certainly do not need you to put my details into an app like 'Wooed and Won.' I mean, what a ridiculous name. What do they know about how to match anybody in real life? I bet they end up pairing me with some physics nerd who couldn't get a date if his life depended on it. That app is probably full of cheating husbands and the kind of guys that nobody would go near with a ten-foot pole!"

"Take a breath before you pass out, you're turning purple! They don't do the matching on this one. I know how fussy you are, and I've given up on pairing you off with anyone, but this might be cool. You browse the site, and you see what interests you," she teased me, clearly not moved one bit by my outburst.

She wasn't even trying to control her laughter. That just made me want to throttle her even more. Alison is great, really. She's my best friend and I adore her, but sometimes she gets these crazy ideas in her head. Most people would just shove them to one side, but no, my kooky and cute buddy just has to act on them.

"You work too hard, and you don't ever see anyone but me. For God's sake Lucy, you're only twenty-two! You need a life. You can't keep living like a hermit! We are supposed to be out there having fun, meeting guys, getting swept off our feet!"

I growled at her and she laughed again. "Alison, I don't have time for fun or casual encounters, let alone a crappy app which will just waste more of my time. I don't have enough clients as it is, and if I don't keep hustling I will never make this business pay."

Alison threw up her hands at me in despair.

"I need to do this Ali. I love my interior decorating work, but it cost me a lot of money to take my exams, and you know I'm still trying to finish my postgrad work off – which means more fees, and more materials for my portfolio work. I am really struggling to make ends meet as it is. If I take any time out right now I will lose everything I have worked so hard for," I said and sighed.

"Honey, I know just how hard you work. I see you every night hunched over those books and magazines, sketching and making up mood boards for your classes and your clients, but look at you." She got up from our battered couch and dragged me to the mirror in the hallway. "Look, you are skin and bones, and have bags under your eyes that a new mom of quintuplets would be proud of."

I tried not to look because deep down I knew she was right. I'd been avoiding reflective surfaces for months now. I wasn't taking care of myself and it showed. My once lustrous and curly auburn hair was tied back in a greasy ponytail. I hadn't been able to afford to get it cut in over six months. And my clothes were hanging off me. I so rarely found the time during the day to eat at all, let alone make a healthy choice if I did, and my skin looked pale and gray from all the time I spent trapped indoors.

"Okay, so I'm a bit of a fixer-upper, but couldn't you have at least let me get fixed before you signed me up to a dating app?"

"Just take a little look through. You can't keep mooning over the past and letting it get in the way of your future, Luce."

She had never dared to be so blatant before. There had been hints, sure, but she had never come out and said it like that. She was talking about Cole of course. Just one of the taboo subjects around me, and I hated her for making me think about him, about any of that stuff from back then.

Gorgeous Cole Kent who had made high school bearable, who hadn't left my side when my mom died of cancer, who had been the cutest and sweetest boy I never got to kiss more than once. My best friend, my rock, and the guy everyone else would have to live up to and never could – right up until he became my stepbrother and my entire world crumbled into dust.

Alison kissed me on the forehead and pulled on her coat. "Think about it Luce, maybe it's time to let go of the past and at least have some fun in the present. And don't yell at me again," she said hurriedly as she saw me about to try and defend myself. "I know what happened back then, and I know how much it hurt you. But, you can't let it fester any longer. For God's sake, get some help, go out on a date or two, and build a life that makes you happy so you can really leave it in the past if that is truly where you want your family to belong. Stop dragging it all around with you like a giant ball and chain all the time. Not for me, but for yourself. You don't deserve to be so damned unhappy all the time."

Her words penetrated my weak defenses. God, I hated it when she was right.

She opened the door, and looked at me tenderly. "I love you Luce, and you deserve better than you are letting yourself have. I've got to go to work, but think about what I've said while I'm gone, please?"

I nodded, but knew that this conversation would be shoved down into the file marked 'Just Don't Go There' in my head, at least not yet.

I slunk back into the living room, and crashed heavily onto the couch. Thoughts about Cole started to escape the confines of the locked box where I had imprisoned my entire past. I tried to banish them back into the black hole, but the harder I tried the more they just kept bursting like bubbles in front of my tired eyes.

He had been one of those guys who was just simply perfect. Though deep down inside beat the heart of an all-out geek, he was also a bit of a jock, a swimmer. He had sun-kissed skin all year round from being in the pool every day, his back a perfect V of muscular perfection. His washboard abs made everybody drool.

All the girls were hot for him, including me, despite his reputation for being super smart and an IT wiz. But, he was also the kindest and sweetest boy alive and my very best friend. God dammit, I missed him so much more than I ever wanted to admit.

Mom, Dad, and I had been so close. I think when you are an only child – especially one your parents described as a miracle baby following years of struggling to conceive – your relationship with them is much more intense. My mom was the best, and she always had time for me. She encouraged me to develop my love of art and crafts, let me help when she decorated the house, and made me believe that anything was possible if you wanted it badly enough. Dad, a carpenter by trade, taught me how to use hammers and drills, and inspired me to use up any spare wood lying around in the garage to create whatever I wanted.

Our home was full of laughter, and love. Oh, how I longed to go back to that time, when everything was simple and uncomplicated... and when I had Cole.

But then the cancer came.

It permeated every minute of each day, as we watched Mom grow weaker and more unwell. And then she was gone, and I didn't know what to do anymore. I was a shell, held carefully together by Cole's tenderness, but then he was taken away from me too.

All because of my dad and Stephanie, Cole's Mom.

Dad was just as lost as I was, and if it hadn't been for Aunty Steph – who was not really an aunt, she was my Mom's best friend – I think he would have disappeared wholly into his grief, too. And soon, everything changed; too much and too quick, and there was no way back.

Ali was right about that. I had to stop letting it take me over; it was in the past and I needed to find a way to make it stay there. Therapy would probably be the best bet, but dating suddenly seemed an easier option and cheaper at that.

I picked up my cell and clicked on the "Wooed and Won" app Alison had downloaded onto it. I grinned when I saw she had chosen a great picture of me, thank god. It was the one from my graduation from the Rhode Island School of Design. I looked so happy and proud. It was everything I had ever dreamed of, and I had worked so very hard for it – but as I looked closely at the snapshot, my grin faded, and I realized there was a haunted look in my eyes. I remembered seeing my fellow students with their families all around them that day, and having had a tiny pang of regret that my own would never know that I had achieved my dreams. I had convinced myself that it was their loss, but even now I was beginning to think it just might be mine.

I shook my head free of the memories and flicked the screen nonchalantly, scrolling past the list of names and pictures. I had been so right, and almost exited the app in disgust. Most were either complete sleaze balls or absolute nerds. A plethora of heavy-framed glasses and Lotharios with hairy chests and medallions gazed back at me. I laughed. What was that about in this day and age?

This was no way to meet the love of your life, like picking out a dress from a catalogue. The analogy made me smile. I so often tried to buy clothes online or from a catalogue because I hated to shop, but I sent most of them back because they just didn't fit, or weren't as nice as they'd looked in the pictures. It would appear that online dating would be much the same – yet if these guys looked any worse in the flesh, or were even more boring than their profiles suggested, yikes!

Just one profile stood out, a man of mystery it would seem. There was no picture, and that should have had me worried. I couldn't help but wonder why a guy who sounded so confident and happy would leave his picture blank, but "Apollo" had chosen to do so. I rolled my eyes at the screen name he'd given himself, but couldn't help feel even more intrigued. Maybe he wanted to stand out amongst the crowd, or maybe he was even sadder than the other nerds – and that would be saying something!

I studied the rest of his profile; it was sweet and engaged. He liked literature, and not just bro action thriller stuff. My eyebrows shot up as I read that he claimed to love Vanity Fair and Wuthering Heights, two of my all-time favorites. But maybe he was just bullshitting.

He listed that he enjoyed cooking and long walks, as well as being by the sea and water sports as passions. I could do without the long walks part, but I loved being by the sea. It always brought back happier memories of day trips when I was tiny. Sure he said he loved computers, and that had a few warning signals flashing in my mind, but I tried to remember that Cole had liked computers too, and he had been great in every way. Apollo was even a postgrad like me, though he surprisingly didn't say what he was studying, just that he was at the university here in Providence.

I couldn't help but read his details and think that he sounded too good to be true. I nibbled at my lower lip as my finger hovered over the little contact button.

There was no harm in at least saying hello, was there?

3

COLE

I jumped three feet in the air as my new cell vibrated loudly in my pocket, bashing my head hard on the roof of the truck. I'd only picked up the new phone yesterday, a little bonus gift from Callie for doing the work on the app, but I hadn't had the time to work out the most basic of functions on it yet.

Mom told me to sit down with the manual and work it out, but I had laughed at her – it was such a female thing to do. I'd figure it out. One cell is pretty much like the next after all. I seemed to have lost my gadget obsession as I got older. In the past a new toy would have been dissected in moments, but I was just happy if they did what I needed them to now.

I rubbed my sore head distractedly as I yanked the phone out of my jeans pocket, struggling to make sure my change didn't follow it out and all over the floor. I really needed new pants, or to hit the pool a bit more often. Just a few weeks in a demanding desk job, with no time to work out at the gym or the pool, had made me fill out slightly in ways I did not want. Though I was grateful that my torso still remained defined as ever, it wouldn't take too much to get back into shape.

The shocking buzzing had heralded the arrival of an email from "Wooed and Won."

That will absolutely be the last time I bet on Jake being prepared to eat anything, I thought.

After eating wings drenched in a cayenne pepper sauce and even a whole basketful of fried locusts, he had balked on a simple green olive. Apparently they were his kryptonite. I was sticking by my side of the deal though, but Callie had predicted pretty accurately that there was indeed an army of people who didn't have the courage to ask anyone out on a date, and somehow her advertising had found all of them.

The app wasn't exactly bursting with gorgeous, smart and sassy women. It was more of a haven for the quiet, clever, and unusual. Weeding out the candidates was proving tough. Sure they were smart, but social skills and hobbies in common seemed to be zilch, *nada*! I had already been forced to endure three of the worst dates of my entire life. I just had one left to go on and my end of the bet would be held up. I prayed that whoever had mailed me this time would be more interesting than the best of the bunch so far: a thirty-year-old librarian who collected and crocheted doilies.

Not wanting to crash, I decided to check it out later and jumped out of the cab of my beaten-up old truck and crunched my way up the gravel drive to the back gate.

The sun was still out, the sky a haze of pinks and darkening oranges as it dipped lower towards the horizon, and that meant that everyone would be out back. They'd enjoying the small swimming pool Tom had managed to get for a huge discount when a client at his work had offered to trade skills. Since its arrival the family had barely been found inside the house, they were so excited to have such a luxury. Tom and my mom were always out on the lounge chairs sipping mojitos most days now. Hopefully there would be a few beers in the cooler too.

Today was most definitely not a cocktail kind of a day. My mouth watered at the thought of the promise of a crisp cold beer that'd soon be hitting my taste buds. It had been a rough journey home to Newton. The traffic had been insane as I had crossed the border between Rhode Island and Massachusetts, the usual hour-and-a-half trip taking closer to three hours, and after three all-nighters and two weeks of manic days at the office, I was beat.

My second year as a summer intern at the DA's office in Providence was proving to be a real eye opener. As an assistant to the Assistant District Attorney I was the lowest of the low, but the experience would look great on my CV. I'd always wanted to be a lawyer, a public defender in fact. I think everyone has the right to a fair trial, and a good defense.

I was picking up a lot about how to build a solid case, and though I was currently on the "wrong" side, I was learning how to make things tough for your opponents, but it was damn hard work! The office often dealt with some pretty heinous crimes, and we were currently trying to get a guy put behind bars where he belonged after he had brutally attacked a convenience store owner and taken every penny he had. He had a great attorney though, and his minions were making things tough for us, trying to bury us with all kinds of motions and wads of paper a mile high. Coming home on the weekends when I could and being with my family helped me unwind, though it always felt like something, someone, was missing.

"Cole, will you take me to the zoo tomorrow, please?" Morgan announced. My adorable half-sister emerged from the pool, dripping wet in a bright red bathing suit with an open-mouthed Elmo emblazoned across the front of it. She held her arms up to me, wanting me to pick her up and swing her around.

"Sure, but don't you want Mommy and Daddy to take you?"

She shook her tight curly head at me. "You're more fun, and you always buy me ice cream," she said thinking about her answer seriously.

I couldn't help but laugh. I hadn't been sure that I was ready for a new sister at seventeen, but I adored her even though she reminded me so much of her other half-sibling growing up. The same auburn hair, the bubbly personality, the huge, deep green eyes. It was like we still had a little bit of Lucy here with us. The gap could never be filled, but it sure helped having the munchkin around to keep us all busy.

I picked her up and twirled her round as she giggled maniacally.

"I'd better go and get changed. I'll be back in a moment," I explained as I set her down and her cute Cupid's bow mouth began to pout. I ruffled her wet hair, and gave her a quick kiss. "I won't be long."

"Promise?" she asked.

"Cross my heart and hope to die," I replied without hesitation and stuck out my pinky finger. Morgan quickly shot out her own pinky and wrapped it around mine.

"Deal," she said and smiled from ear to ear, revealing her dimples once more and then sprinted as fast as she could back into the pool.

"Hey Cole," Mom said warmly as she emerged with a tray filled with iced drinks.

"They look good," I said salivating at the sight of the long-necked beer bottles covered in condensation. Mom laughed.

"How long are you staying this time honey?"

"Why, do you want to get rid of me already?" I teased her, knowing she would have been happy for all of us to live at home until the day we died.

"Never, but I know you. You'll want your space again soon."

I had to admit that once Morgan had arrived, as much as I loved her, it had gotten a lot noisier and harder to pay attention to my studies and get anything done at home. When the opportunity came to go to UCLA and then to law school at Roger Williams University on full scholarships, I had jumped at them. UCLA, in particular, had been a long way from home and it had been tough being so far away, but it had meant that while Tom had scoured the East Coast schools for Lucy, I had used my weekends to do the same on the West Coast.

When I graduated in the top five of my class, I had won a place at Harvard Law which had been a little closer to home, but the fees had been out of my reach, and with all the competition there had been no financial aid. Roger Williams was a bit farther away and obviously hadn't got anywhere near as good a reputation, but the scholarship and the money I got from the work from Callie and Jake's company, Glitch, meant I could afford a nice little apartment to myself. It also helped that I wasn't too far from where they'd set up their offices in Providence. Having my two best buddies nearby, after two years where the entire continent had separated us for most of the year, was definitely a plus point for Rhode Island.

Jake thought Rhode Island was the best place in the world, and had missed it while we had all been at UCLA together. He couldn't wait to get home and when his and Callie's first collaboration started to make them serious money he jumped at the chance to drop out and head back. It suddenly hit me that Callie must truly love him, otherwise why would the sexy Californian not have insisted that she return to her beachfront home on the West Coast?

No, she hadn't even stopped to think about it, had just upped and left to work with him back east. How had I been so blind? Maybe a bit of that vanity again, like Jake I had always assumed that if she had a crush on anyone that it was probably me. Well, I would do a bit of matchmaking when I got back and push the idiots into each other's arms where they belonged. Looking back over the years of our friendship, I wondered why I hadn't picked up on it before - there were just so many clues!

"Just tonight, sadly Mom. I have to get back to the office by Sunday afternoon. We're having a final strategy meeting before the trial starts on Monday."

"Then we had best make the most of you. Go and get changed, you must be sweltering. I'm going to try and tear your sister away from the pool and get her to bed. I only let her stay up this long because she knew you were coming. There was no point in even trying, she would have been escaping every five minutes to see if you were here yet! So, if you hear any screams it's probably me," she said.

"Well don't make a liar out of me. I promised Morgan I'd be back to play," I replied.

"Oh, fine then," she laughed and rolled her eyes. "She can stay up a while longer. Go get your trunks on."

I nodded and ran up the stairs and dove into the shower to rinse the accumulation of travel sweat off me.

The shower was cool, and I felt refreshed when I emerged. I pulled on some swimming shorts, and picked up my cell. I remembered the email and quickly pulled it up. It was a notification of a new member who would like to chat. I sighed heavily and clicked on the link to go to the site, not expecting much but figuring this could maybe be my final date requirement and then this hell would all be over.

I was not prepared for the shock I got when I saw the profile picture of the woman who wanted to maybe hook up with me and was forced to sit down on the end of the bed.

In a swirl of conflicting emotions, my spirits soared and my heart sank as I studied the face before me on the screen.

On the one hand, I realized that this candidate could never be my final date to end the bet. No, I'd still need to keep looking for her. I sighed with mild frustration at the prospect of another evening in the company of the lost and unwanted of Rhode Island.

But on the other, as I gazed into the depths of the emerald eyes of this enquirer, hypnotized by her absolute perfection, I was overwhelmed with relief.

Lucy was alive, and by some stroke of luck or fate or both, she was almost within my reach for the first time in years. Closing my eyes, tears threatening, I took a deep breath and finally allowed all the worry and pain to slowly disperse from my body.

Yet I knew that it would definitely take much more than a week of emails and texts to build this one's trust to meet me for a date.

I could feel my heartbeat pound against my chest.

Thank fuck that I now knew where she was. I'd always tried to keep my hopes in check over the years, never really believing that I'd find her, and yet here she was beaming at me on the screen.

She looked just as spunky, and clearly as determined as ever. The picture showed her in a cap and gown, so I knew she'd graduated college even without family support. You had to admire that.

What a girl Lucy Rivers had always been. Her face was as familiar as my own once, but now I could see the clearer lines and less rounded features of a woman, not a girl. She looked harder, tougher than I remembered her, but her cat-like eyes were still filled with the sadness I had seen in them when she'd left here five years ago with hatred in her heart.

But still, even through the haunted look in her eyes, she looked fantastic. I could feel the usual pull that her closeness had always left me with as a teenager, an ache in my groin and a desire I could never shake. And all this from a tiny profile photo... I could only imagine the effect she would have on me if I were to see her in person.

Yet, how could I possibly let her know who I really was?

She would run a mile, but I had to know she was okay, had to try and rebuild the trust we had once shared. She was the only woman who had ever gotten me so hot and horny I couldn't think straight, and trying to maintain our lifelong friendship had been tough as we had blundered through our teen years.

God, I remembered that glorious, summer night like it was yesterday. We had so nearly taken everything to the next level... and that incredible kiss still tormented me to this very day.

The perfect moment when we had finally been alone had been unexpectedly interrupted by the news that would change everything, forever. I could still recall the frustration I had felt, my cock so hard and eager, and my body feeling so robbed of the sensation of her soft breasts pressed up against my hard chest, her silky skin under my fingers.

Even now, just thinking of that night alone in her bedroom made my cock twitch with excitement. Oh, I wanted her... still do.

I pushed the urge to explore the memory further as I tried to figure out my next move. My head felt dizzy with indecision.

I should tell Lucy's dad, Tom, and my Mom that Lucy was okay, that I'd inadvertently found her. They'd want to know she was fine and had fulfilled her dream of being an interior designer. They had a right to know, I told myself, but an almost imperceptible inkling urged me to keep the information under wraps for now.

Guilt swirled in my belly. Tom had been worried out of his mind for years, had tried to trace her, but without enough money to hire a private detective we had come up against every kind of barrier. The police had deemed her old enough to make her own decisions. Her leaving home had broken the poor man's heart. Mom had tried to console him, and the arrival of Morgan just six months later had probably helped him to learn to live with the absence of his beloved first daughter, but he had never come to terms with her being gone. It had been so hard for them both when they got married, not having her there, not having her blessing.

It had been tough for me too. I hated the idea that the girl I adored was now my stepsister, but I didn't take it half as badly as Lucy did. To her my mom and her dad getting married was a betrayal she simply could not get past.

I wondered if she was still angry, or if maybe I could find a way now to be the friend she had so needed then, but that my idiotic, hormonal teenage brain couldn't bring itself to be at the time. I'd been angry too. I had wanted her too badly. The new sudden change from best friends – and almost more – into being siblings had made it insanely hard to be around her, and my desperate attempts to make her listen, not just react, had made her push me further away too.

But unlike Luce, I had known that Joanna, her mom, had schemed to ensure her husband would be cared for and loved by her best friend even on her death bed. And I was stubborn. I couldn't, and wouldn't condemn my mom, or Tom for doing what Jo had so begged them to do – not even for Lucy.

They deserved to be happy too, and I know they found solace from the pain they had both been through in each other, and real love grew between them. It wasn't just about Jo's dying wish; it was about what made them both feel whole again. I would never want to deny anyone that feeling. I hoped every day that I would find my better half so I could be whole again too. And here she was, in Providence, Rhode Island - and suddenly the mountain I had to climb to gain her trust again seemed even higher than when I had no clue where she was!

4
LUCY

I still couldn't believe that I sent a message to "Apollo." Hell, I must have been possessed. I didn't have time to date, and I certainly didn't need anyone in my life that couldn't even be up front enough about something as simple as his real name.

He probably won't even respond, I mused. And laughed at myself for getting so caught up over it. I needed to concentrate on my marketing. If I didn't find some new clients, and pronto, I would soon be joining the unemployment line and I was not ready for that.

I was almost nearly finished on my final project for my postgraduate degree, and the client was extremely happy – thank god. However, unlike my normal jobs, there wouldn't be a juicy fat check waiting at the end of this one. I was only able to charge my material costs since it was for my qualifications.

And yet, my bank account was crying out for funds. I quickly checked my balance through an app and sighed when the familiar numbered appeared on the screen. I was down to my last fifty dollars. Did I really believe that just by checking the balance for the umpteenth time that day would make the number magically grow? Bah. I had to figure something out quick, because I had no idea if I could make it stretch until the end of the month if I didn't manage to get another job lined up for when I finished my current one.

I felt like I'd tried everything. I'd delivered more flyers around all the rich residential districts than my feet could cope with – my heels had been covered in blisters by the time I finally made it home. I'd also sent out emails and letters, even tried calling every business within a fifty-mile radius, and yet nobody seemed to be hiring.

Where was my knight in shining armor or fairy godmother? I just needed one person to give me a break who preferably also had some great contacts. Was that too much to ask for?

If I could only get my foot in the door somewhere. I'd dreamed of getting to tackle the new tech company in the financial district's head office. It was a fantastic old Victorian block, and they hadn't done anything to it since they'd moved in... neglected it if you asked me. I'd walked past it a few times and the building has practically screamed out to me for some love and attention. A job like that could keep me in work for months, if not years. If only I knew how to get hold of one of the directors, but they seem to be guarded closer than the President. Nobody got near them, or in through their heavily guarded door. Believe me, I tried. Apparently they were geniuses and did not take kindly to unannounced visitors that tried to slip in with the lunch crowd. I'd have to find another way, I considered.

The front door opened, Ali entered in a bit of a whirlwind and discarded her belongings on our small shabby chic table. She took one look at me and sighed. "Okay grumpy, get your coat. I'm taking you out for dinner. I need a great big steak and I do not want to eat alone."

Ali's voice was her 'not to be argued with' one. Well tough, I thought, I was going to argue anyway.

"I am not a charity case, and I can't afford to eat in, let alone out, so sorry, you are on your own, sister," I said in a huff, even though the idea of a big porterhouse dripping with blood made my taste buds tingle.

"This isn't charity. I need your advice. I need iron, and therefore I need you and I need a steak. Get your butt away from that desk and come out with me. If not I'll get it as takeout and bring it home so the smell of it fills every bit of the apartment and you'll be forced to join me."

I frowned while I struggled to keep a smile at bay. Alison knew me way too well. I can't for the life of me resist the smell of food. She had weakened my resolve to accept her charity on too many occasions to know just how to push my buttons.

"You tease! Okay, okay. Do I have enough time to have a quick shower and wash my hair? I think I still have paint everywhere from work."

"Sure, I love you Luce, but I would prefer it if you didn't smell of paint thinner. It kind of ruins the taste of the beef. So sure, use my shampoo if you like."

I grinned a little shamefacedly at her. You couldn't put anything by her; she never missed a damn thing. I had run out of toiletries a few weeks ago and had finally worked my way through all the tiny little ones that we had lying around for guests to use and was now just going for the "get everything wet and hope for the best" approach.

Thirty or so minutes later, with my stomach rumbling eagerly, we were speed walking to Fleming's on West Exchange Street. We couldn't get there fast enough.

It was pricey, but so good. Their thirty-two ounce Porterhouse to share, slathered with their special porcini mushroom rub was quite possibly the closest thing to heaven I have ever experienced, culinary speaking.

We had splurged on one just twice before: on the day I graduated two years ago; and when Alison got her first job at the Trinity Repertory Company eight months ago. She was a great actress, and they had loved her so much that they had kept her on permanently. She had barely missed a show for them in that time and she loved the range of things she got to do on stage. It was a rare night that she had off from the theater. I was glad, and grateful, that she wanted to share this one with me.

"Okay, I need your advice," she started once we had placed our order and been presented with our bottle of Chilean merlot. I sipped my glass and enjoyed the sensation of the warm fruity wine moving over my tongue and down my throat. "I've been offered the lead in our next production."

"Wow, that is amazing, congratulations! Why on earth do you need my advice about that?" I asked, pleased as anything for her and more than a little bit confused.

"Anthony will be playing the male lead," she said with a big sigh.

"Oh, shit..."

"Right?" she replied.

Anthony had broken her heart. They had dated all through college, been real hot and heavy. She had thought that they were headed toward an engagement at least, when he had announced that he'd been offered a part in an off-Broadway play and that he intended to go alone so he could enjoy 'everything he could' about the entire experience. It had been crystal clear what he had meant by *everything*, that he wanted to play the field and fuck his co-stars, or anyone else for that matter, if the opportunity should arise.

"Well, I suppose the question is: Do you still love him?"

I'd always believed in getting straight to the point of other people's problems. It cuts out all the bullshit and gets it all dealt with so much quicker. I know I should be the same about my own crap, but somehow I seem to do nothing but dither and brush my stuff under the rug. Maybe it was time to stop doing that, and maybe take a bit of the advice I would be happy to offer anyone I love.

Alison looked at me for a moment, then her eyes darted away, and her mouth made tiny little movements as she thought about the question. I waited as she considered her answer, not wanting to push.

"I don't think so. I mean, I know he is a complete prick, and I *so* don't want to waste another moment of my life on him, but I guess what I am afraid of is that I just don't know, and won't know until I see him again."

I nodded my understanding. How would I feel if I ever saw Cole again? Cole wasn't remotely like Alison's ex, but still how could I know for sure deep down what I obsessed over all these years was actually accurate and true?

You know exactly what you'd feel, a little voice inside me screamed.

"Hey Ali, trust me on this one, if you are in love with a guy, truly in love with him, just thinking about him even after five years will still give you goose bumps. And the idea of dating anyone else will seem like it is a betrayal of his memory, and whenever you let your guard down and let him into your head you will struggle for days to put him back in the box marked 'Do Not Open.' You got any of that going on?"

"I am utterly glad to say that no, I do not have any of that going on about him Luce, but sounds like you still do about Cole. Sorry I opened up that can of worms for you honey."

She frowned, and I saw real concern in her eyes. Ali is one of those rarities, a black-haired Celtic beauty, with long lashes that frame the most vivid baby blues. She is tiny and petite, and would make the perfect elf or pixie if she only had pointy ears.

"Nope, we aren't going there. Tonight is about you and your shit, not mine!" I tried to sound jokey, but just the mention of his name already had me distracted. Yeah, I knew exactly how sending the email to Apollo had made me feel like the absolute worst person alive. How could I even think about replacing Cole in my heart?

Thankfully the steak arrived just in time to diffuse the tension, and we ate heartily, both of us ravenous. It was delicious, and my body reveled in the massive burst of nutrition. I struggled to finish my share. My stomach had shrunk so badly from the months of barely getting enough in to keep me going. But I was determined to do so. I knew I needed it, all of it. Finally done, and only a few tiny droplets of grease remaining on our plates, feeling bloated and uncomfortable, we both leaned back in our chairs and giggled at each other.

We knew the look of shock we'd get from the waiter when he returned to collect our empty plates. We were both pretty small and slight, and yet could eat our own weight in anything and never seem to gain a pound. I had been curvy before my financial troubles, but everything now was pretty angular and sharp. Ali was still pretty feminine, looking like something ethereal and insubstantial almost, with her cropped hair and upturned nose. But we were both pretty active because of the work we did, and we burned through everything super quick.

"So, how is the hunt for clients going then?" Ali asked me as we finished off the bottle of wine.

"Not great, but I'm sure I'll find something."

"Please, will you let me at least make sure there is food in the fridge for you Luce? I'm getting really worried about you. I'll be earning more as the lead, and I can afford to help you out. It isn't as if you didn't do the same for me when I was trying to get my first acting gigs. Please quit being so proud?"

With a full tummy for the first time in weeks, it would have been so easy to try and pretend I was fine, to let my damned stupid pride get in the way – but I knew in my heart that she was right. I couldn't continue to work this hard on nothing. I nodded at her reluctantly.

"Sure, thanks Ali."

My cell pinged. I was grateful for the distraction. We could hopefully change the subject. The screen flickered into life and I saw a message from Apollo.

"Anything interesting?" Ali inquired, curious as she took in the wary look on my face.

"Well, you know you signed me up to that dating site, and I told you it wasn't happening?"

She nodded with a definite gleam in her eye, clearly excited that I had done something about it.

"And? What did you do?" she squealed.

"I sent a message to a guy."

Ali's face transformed, grinning like a mad woman and made a show of clapping her hands together. "Well, tell me more... tell me everything!"

"He calls himself Apollo. He seemed okay. At least he's responded." I was trying so hard to sound nonchalant, but just seeing his name had sent shivers through me and I suddenly felt a little clammy.

"So are you going to open it and tell me what he says?"

"I'm not sure I can," I said as I almost dropped the cell, my hands were shaking so badly. "I wasn't expecting him to get back to me. I don't know if I'm ready for this." I could feel my heart racing really fast now, and my breathing had gotten more rapid and I was almost gasping for air.

"Want me to have a look? Remember you don't have to reply, don't even have to open it if you don't want to Luce. But I think it might help you if you do. You need to work through this, once and for all." She took my hand and held it tightly. She had been my only family for such a long time, and I was so lucky she was my friend. She put up with all my chaotic behavior and screwed up moods.

And to think how easily we may have passed each

other by. She was a cool drama student and I a nervous freshman, but the design school and the drama school kids all hung out at the same bars, though at different ends, or even floors if that were possible. We met on a particularly drunken night at The Avery, and had almost come to blows over who would get the last free booth. Alison had won, her vomiting taking the decision making out of both our hands. I pulled her hair back from her face and waited patiently while she tossed her cookies. It was one of those things that just meant you left the bathroom the best of friends.

I shook my head now though. She was right. This was something I had to do for myself.

"Okay, here we go… let's hope he's not a weirdo."

I clicked on the message to open it up. I started reading, and his gentle words soon soothed my fears. He really did sound like a nice guy. My breathing began to slow again as he talked about his half-sister, and how much he'd enjoyed taking her to the zoo that day. A smile began to break my tight features.

"He seems great," I said simply.

She squeezed my hand and poured the last bit of the wine into our glasses.

"Good."

5

COLE

I have never been a big fan of talking on the phone, and though I appear pretty confident I am quite shy in person. I find it hard to relax around new people, and around girls I usually find it impossible. I've always let others put it down to the fact I am a bit of a nerd, I study super hard, and love Star Trek and Star Wars, comics, and all that "Big Bang Theory" kind of stereotypically geeky stuff. The only people who know that it is only part of who I am are Jake and Callie. But as the days go by and I chat more and more with Lucy online I realize that most of it is just because there was a big Lucy shaped hole in my heart that I didn't want to fill with just anyone.

I felt guilty as hell that she didn't know it was me at the end of the emails, but I had no clue how to tell her now. I should have done it right away, but with my mind on the trial and not wanting to scare her away I just put it off, and off, and now I couldn't bear the thought that she would run from me again. I liked having her back in my life. Her quirky way of looking at the world, her worries, and her joys made me feel just the way I always did back when we were teenagers. Work was crazy, but getting in to find a message from her made it all worth it. I looked forward to the evenings when we messaged back and forth all night. I grabbed a beer and sat down with my phone and pretended she was right there in the room with me.

But not tonight, I thought. Tonight my friends have stamped their feet and demanded I stop being a recluse and go out on the town. I heard the honk of Jake's classic Mustang downstairs, and hit return on the last message I would be able to send her that night, grabbed my coat and ran down the stairs.

Callie managed to get us tickets to go and see the Red Hot Chili Peppers. I have loved them forever, and used to force Luce to rock out with me to every album they ever made. Even now they are still one of the greatest bands to see live, and I had been looking forward to the gig so much. Yet, now I feel as if I could take it or leave it, and just stay home and keep chatting with her. She is out herself tonight, so I may as well go, I thought. I would be a pretty sad fuck if I just sat in and mooned over her instead.

"So, how is the hunt for the final date going?" Callie asked with a glint in her eye as I scrambled into the back seat.

"As a matter of fact I have a date tomorrow with a personal trainer called Magda. She is about six foot six, is a competitive body builder, and quite frankly scares the shit out of me. I'm going to try and make sure I am so obnoxious that she never wants to see me again!" I winked at her.

"Don't you dare piss off any of our customers, Kent. Make her feel super special even if you hate every minute or I will have your guts my friend." A mean look crossed over her lovely face and I laughed.

"Cole couldn't be mean to anyone, even if there was a gun to his head. Gentleman to the core Callie, you know that. Now leave him be. You have three women who have already given us great reviews and recommended the app to plenty of their friends because of the dates he took them out on. He isn't going to suddenly become a complete shit, even if he wanted to be," Jake said at her pouting face.

"Maybe I need to develop a bit more of the 'treat 'em mean' thing. Clearly being such a nice guy isn't working for me!" I joked, and between us Callie's face began to return to her usual perkily smiley self.

"No, don't you change for anyone sugar. You're perfect as you are."

"Aw, shucks Cal, you'll make me blush! Now, what have you crazy kids been up to this week? Any dirty gossip for me?"

"Change would be a fine thing buddy," Jake snorted. "We work, we eat – occasionally if she lets me have a moment to myself – and we sleep. Nothing left after that."

"*Tsk, tsk* and you two yell at me for working too hard! You need to maybe look up from your laptops occasionally and see what is happening all around you, and especially under your noses," I said cryptically.

I saw Jake's eyebrow rise quizzically in the rear view mirror and I winked at him. His bushy eyebrows furrowed with a look of warning. I chuckled to myself. Nope, I was not going to keep his secret any longer, especially as I was pretty certain I had worked out Callie's too.

The gig was loud and Jake had gotten us great seats, but it was crowded and hot in the arena. I found myself feeling hemmed in, and uncomfortable just being there. God, I was turning into an old man, wanting a bit of peace and quiet and desperate to hear from Lucy again.

I headed out to the bar, leaving my friends bouncing frenetically to the great tracks. With a plastic cup of beer in my hand I walked to a relatively quiet spot by the huge glass walls. I looked out over the city and sighed; it was torturous having Lucy back in my life, nearly within my grasp and yet totally untouchable at the same time.

Guilt washed over me. I knew I had to tell her the truth sometime, tell her who I really was. As I considered my options I took a sip of my beer and turned back toward the bar. A head of auburn curls caught my eye. I could've sworn it was Lucy, but I knew it was only wishful thinking. I was conjuring her up only because she was on my mind pretty much 24/7.

But even though I had my doubts I had to make sure. I chased the slender back through the crowd, losing her momentarily. Gazing anxiously around me I spotted a pert figure sauntering towards the arena doors, two cups of beer in her hands. She turned briefly as if she felt my eyes on her back. A cute co-ed with big blue eyes and a mischievous twinkle grinned at me. She went to move toward me and talk. I sighed and turned back to my quiet spot by the windows.

I have had so many moments like that over the years,

and it was never her. Maybe I should give up, and should leave her in peace. Just fade back out of her life again; she never needs to know who I was.

"Hey, you okay? You took so long I got worried," I hear Callie's drawl asking me gently. "Did you think you'd seen her again?"

"Just a cute girl," I admitted dejectedly.

"You'll find her."

"I already have."

"Wait. What? You found her? Where? How? Why didn't you tell us?"

I sighed, unable to put my thoughts into words.

"Oh, I'm sorry hon... I shouldn't bombard you like that. But is she okay?"

"Yeah, she's fine. Great even. She's on 'Wooed and Won' – but as always I have made a complete mess of it all, and she has no clue that I am me and when she finds out she is going to hate me all over again."

Callie frowned. "Cole, from what you've told me, I don't think she's ever truly hated you. Quite the opposite really, and maybe she misses you and her family just as much as all of you miss her. Maybe she'll be mad to begin with, but if she loves you even a tiny bit she'll find a way to forgive all of you."

"I wish I could be so optimistic Callie, but she was so angry."

"You have to try. Life sucks when you don't take chances my friend."

I could have laughed at the irony. Here was a girl who worked day in and day out by the side of the man I was pretty sure she adored as much as I did Luce, and yet had never so much as made a half-hearted pass at him.

"You gonna take your own advice Cal?" I asked her, turning the tables. I didn't want to talk about my shit any more. She looked stunned.

"Wh...wh...what do you mean by that?" she stuttered, knowing full well what I was implying.

"Come on, your secret is out. It's so obvious you love Jake, and that he loves you and yet the pair of you skate around it as if it simply wasn't there." Callie's mouth dropped open. "He shoots me dirty looks when I hint that he likes you, you do the same when I hint you like him. For fuck's sake, will the two of you just do it and get rid of the hideous 'will they, won't they' soap opera that is our lives?"

"Oh God, you knew. How long have you known?" she gasped.

"Oh about you, only very recently, but Jake I knew from that very first day. He fell hook line and sinker, but figured that a 'fat fuck like himself would never stand a chance with a babe like you' – his words!"

"He really does love me?" Her face looked so hopeful I couldn't help but give her a big hug.

"Callie, he adores you, now go in there, wrap those inordinately long limbs of yours around that tubby belly of his, kiss him senseless and let him know too. You've got ten minutes to get it out of your systems. Then I'm coming back in. You had better be together, but not all over each other by then. I want to enjoy the rest of the show!"

Callie kissed me and bounced off like a rabbit through the crowd.

I slouched against the glass, my good deed for the day done. At least two people I loved would end this day happy, even if I was still wracked with guilt and had no way to assuage it. I finished my beer, and having given them a whole half hour figured it should be safe to go back in. I could hear the intro to "Under the Bridge" and I wasn't going to miss that. Luce had loved it, had played it over and over again, so much so that I had almost come to hate it – but now it always made me feel close to her somehow.

My friends were standing so close that even a sheet of paper wouldn't be able to come between them, and were holding hands. But they were just swaying to the music. Clearly Callie had taken my warning to heart. Jake nudged me as I got back to my seat, a look of absolute joy all over his chubby face. I knew it would take a while for it to all sink in, for him to know that it was all real, but it couldn't have happened to a nicer guy. They might not look like they fitted together, but they were so perfect for one another. I just hoped that my own happy ending would work out so easily in the end.

6

LUCY

I cried as I stood in the pit swaying to "Under the Bridge." Sweat and tears mingled on my face and I hoped my waterproof mascara was up for the challenge.

It was the first song Cole ever played me by the Chili Peppers, and I fell in love with it right off the bat. I remember driving him crazy that summer I played it so often. I even made up a cassette with it on loop

When Alison said they would be playing at the Arena I had shelled out for tickets for us both, managing to scrape every single cent I had together for them. It was just one of the reasons I was so broke, but I wanted to be there. There was no way I was going to miss it. She wasn't excited to go, but had come with me anyway. Now here she seemed to be enjoying herself, and was chatting happily with a guy who had accidentally spilled his beer over her in the crush. He was kind of cute, and dressed in his skater boy chic baggy pants he looked perfect for Ali. I watched as she confidently took his number and kissed him on the cheek, then swayed her way back to me.

"God, that poor guy. You didn't have to do the full on languorous walk, Ali. His tongue may never be able to be picked back up off the floor!"

"He enjoyed it then?" she asked irreverently.

"Oh yeah! He definitely enjoyed it. You gonna give him a call?"

"Maybe, I'll give him a couple of days to stew first, though. Keep him interested. He is pretty hot though, don't you think?"

"If you like them young and stupid, then definitely!" I teased.

We both laughed and as the volume and tempo picked up again for "Californication" we fell quiet and just danced. Being out with Ali was great, she got that music was about feeling it and dancing. She was happy to let me just lose myself in it. It was the only time in my life I didn't feel self-conscious and she just joined me in abandoned pleasure, whether she liked the tune or not. She just got on with it and lived. She was good for me that way.

We staggered up the stairs to our apartment, our ears still ringing from band member Flea's stinging bassline and the hot and heavy guitars. We collapsed, exhausted, on the couch.

"I need water!" Ali announced eventually. "Want some?"

I nodded eagerly as she tried to drag herself up from her comfortable disarray and head towards the kitchen. I pulled my phone out of my pocket, and realized I had missed a message in all the noise.

Hey Lucy. Hope you had a good night. Just wanted to check you got home safe. Apollo x

I grinned, and responded.

Fantastic night. Best in years. Went to see the Chilies. Awesome! How was yours?

I had barely put the phone down on the arm of the chair when it pinged again. He was online.

I was at the Chilies too! Wow, what a coincidence. Fucking fantastic right? My two best friends hooked up together, at last! So happy for them, just wish they had got themselves figured out sooner.

That's so cute! My friend hooked up too, she met a cute skater boy, but I just wanted to dance. It helps me forget all my troubles and just be me.

Sounds like a good thing. Hope you don't have too many troubles, Lucy.

Too few clients, not enough money, the usual stuff!

Want me to ask around see if anyone I know wants anything done?

Nah, but thanks for the thought. I'll work it out somehow. Gotta do it myself, you know? I'm exhausted, think I'd better get some rest. Final day on my last project for college. Need to have my critical eye ready! Night Apollo x

Night Lucy, glad you had a good night, and good luck tomorrow. Let me know how it all goes x

I was still lying there clutching my phone to my chest when Ali appeared with two glasses full of icy cold water. I reached for it like a man who'd been stuck in the desert for days. I drank greedily then sunk back down into my comfy spot.

"You have the oddest look on your face Luce," Ali said

perceptively. "You've heard from the mysterious Apollo again haven't you?"

"He just texted to make sure I'd had a good night. He was at the show too, can you believe it? Shame I just missed him, but nice to know he cares enough about me to check I got home okay."

"If I didn't know you better Lucy Rivers, I'd say you were starting to fall for this guy."

"He does seem very lovely, but I'm too scared to meet him. What if he isn't like all the messages? That guy is sweet and caring, wants to know all about me, isn't scared off by the stuff that isn't so great in my life, and seems to really want to help me if he can. What if he turns out to be some kind of pathological liar, a sociopath, or even worse, *married*?"

Ali snorted then composed herself. "Well Luce, you are only ever going to find out if you actually meet him. Wouldn't it be better to do it sooner rather than later so you don't fall too head over heels with his online persona?"

"Wise as always my friend. But I am too tired to make a decision now. I am going to go to bed, and get a good night's sleep so I can get a good score tomorrow."

"I'm gonna crash too. Night, Luce."

THE NEXT MORNING dawned earlier than I wanted it to, and I dragged my butt out of bed unwillingly. Alison had made sure there was plenty of cereal and I gulped down a bowl as I made a sandwich to take with me to work. I would find a way to pay her back for keeping her word and ensuring the fridge was well stocked. I was already starting to feel a lot better for it, and could see my skin getting a little pinker and plumper each day. I grabbed my lunch and ran down the stairs. I nearly missed my bus, but the driver grinned at me and pulled back in so I could scramble aboard.

"Thanks Eddie, boy am I glad it's you and not Sergei this morning. He would have pulled off just to spite me!" Eddie laughed as he took my fare then waited until I was safely seated and pulled off into the busy rush hour traffic.

The journey across town took thirty minutes, and I looked over my mood boards to refresh my mind with all the finishing touches I needed to get done today before my clients got back from their vacation, and my tutor came to check it over at five o'clock. I was nervous and caught myself biting my lip a few times, but having something so practical to keep my mind and hands occupied helped.

My phone vibrated in my pocket and I whipped it out, expecting it to be Alison wishing me luck, but realized there was no way she would be out of bed yet. It was Apollo.

Go get 'em tiger! X

I grinned and put the phone back in my pocket. It was great having someone else in my life again, someone other than Ali who seemed to genuinely care about me. It was strange, but I hadn't realized just how much I needed it, craved it until he showed up. It was almost like having Cole back in my life - someone who just listened, didn't judge, and was always on my side.

I missed him, and I knew I had probably been too

hard on him. How on earth could I have expected him to turn his back on his mom, after everything they had gone through when his dad ran out on them? He had been so sure it was all his fault, and it had taken Steph and me months to make him realize that his dad was the one with the problem, not either of them.

But I still knew I couldn't go back. I wasn't ready to deal with all that yet. It was still so raw. Not just our parents, but the shame that a guy I had wanted so badly to be my boyfriend had seen me day in and day out in that last year, wandering in and out of the bathroom before I'd done my hair, or my face; in my pajamas and the highly embarrassing moments when we'd both burst in on each other in the shower.

But Apollo made me feel the same way he had, safe and cared for, with none of the icky embarrassment stuff. It was nice, and I knew I should give in to his requests to meet but I was just too scared. I didn't even know what he looked like after all. I suddenly had a thought. It might be a way around it all, a way to break the ice and have some fun if he took it well. I grabbed my phone and quickly tapped out the text before I lost my nerve.

Thanks, I hope to be in the mood for celebrating once today is done. If you still want to meet up I think it might be kind of fun, but I have one condition...

What is that one commandment my Lady? Your wish is my command!

I want to see a picture of you. I know you are a little shy, so no trying to send me a stock pic from the net somewhere. I want the picture to show you are standing by either the Elk Monument, or the Roger Williams one. AND I want you to be holding a single red dahlia.

Peculiar request but consider it done! I'll get it over to you by the end of the day. Then maybe we can agree to a time and place at last? :)

We shall see, Mister Apollo, we shall see, I thought as I tucked my phone back into my jeans pocket. A new start, a new guy... a fresh start. Ali had been right. Just the idea of a date with a guy I really liked was definitely improving my mood. I was nervous, sure, but I couldn't wait to meet him in person at last. I just prayed I'd like what I saw in his picture...

7

COLE

"Fuck! What the hell am I going to do, Callie? She wants a picture of me. If she sees a photo of me that's it. If I can at least get her to meet with me I have a hope of convincing her to give me a chance, but if I can't get that far this whole thing is dead on the water!"

I stopped by the Glitch office in the recess for lunch from court. I needed help and Callie was the only person I could think of who might come up with a solution.

"Take a breath. She is a smart cookie your Lucy isn't she? I love the demands of what to include!"

I glared at her. Now was not the time to be amused by my predicament, or to admire how clever Lucy could be.

"Do I need to remind you that you weren't doing so well in your love life before I gave you a nudge? You owe me, MacAllister!" She tried to pull her face into a serious look, but she couldn't keep the smile from her eyes.

"Calm down and don't get your knickers in a twist!"

"Where did that one come from?" Callie had a whole raft of odd expressions.

"Oh, a British aunt. But that's beside the point. The Elk Monument is just around the corner. It is usually a pretty quiet spot. You have any problems whipping your shirt off in public Kent?" I could see where she was going, and I had to admit it was genius.

"No, I don't think so…" I said cautiously. But if it got me out of this predicament, I thought, I'd probably do anything. "I think my body still holds up to photographic scrutiny. But what about the dahlia? What the hell is a dahlia anyway?"

"It is a type of flower you ignoramus. The good thing is there are so many different types of them we are bound to find one somewhere in the city. I'm texting our florist now." Her fingers flew over her phone screen.

"Fuck, you have a florist? For a place you haven't even painted the walls of yet?"

"I know, the irony. But we have just been too busy to even think about décor, but I have to have my flowers."

"Hey, you are a genius as always. I think I can help you out there. Lucy is an interior designer. She's doing her postgrad at the School of Design, and is just about to finish today in fact. She needs clients. She is awesome – well she always used to be when we were kids anyway, I can only imagine how much better she is now she's had five years of formal training too. Could you maybe give her a room or two to work on here? She is playing it down, but I think she's struggling a bit to get clients lined up."

"Hell, she can do the entire building if she's good enough. That should keep her in work for a year or two at least! Aren't you worried she'll find out you pulled strings?"

"There are so many things I am scared shitless about around Lucy, but I can't bear to think of her being short on cash when there is something I can do to help out. Anyway, I'm not going to ask you to definitely give her the job, just invite her to offer a suggestion or something. If you don't like her ideas don't use her, but I can give her a chance at least."

"Done Kent. I'll be subtle."

Her phone rang out with the tones of Eminem and Dido's "Stan."

"We are in luck. Gabby has in fact put red pom-pom dahlias in our foyer display today. Shows what I notice when I come in to work! Let's get out of here, and get this picture taken before you get reamed out by the judge for being back late."

Grabbing the bright red dahlia as we tore through the hallway, Callie pulling me by the hand, we almost knocked Jake over as he came back in from a trip to the bakery down the block.

"Hey, watch the baked goods!" he said. A brief look of concern came over his face as he saw our hands. "You'd better not be stealing my girl, Cole," he said, only half-joking.

"No worries there buddy, she is too damn bossy for me! I'll give her back in ten minutes, she'll tell you all about it then!" Callie kissed him quickly and then carried on dragging me out the door and down the street.

The Elk Monument is exactly what it sounds like: a giant elk on a plinth.

"Okay Kent, shirt off and drape yourself over that," Callie said with a wink.

I looked at her and wondered if I was starting to go

mad. Here I was, a year from finishing law school, working for the DA and about to drape myself half-naked over an elk. If it had been for anyone other than Lucy I would have said forget it, it wasn't worth it. But I knew it was.

I pulled off my tie, stripped out of my shirt and climbed up to lean against the giant beast.

"Well, you kept those well hidden all these years!" Callie said eyeing up my washboard abs. "If I had known about them, Jake wouldn't have stood a chance."

She winked. I knew she didn't mean a word of it. Jake had won her heart because of who he was, not because he had a hot body, that was for certain.

"Nah, I can't compete with the ten donut a day habit that has built Jake's fine physique. I know I will always only ever be second best," I teased. "Now, how do you want me?" She tossed the dahlia to me.

"With a body like that Kent, it doesn't matter what you do with it really, but undo the button on your fly, tuck a hand down just a little and hold the flower between your nipples. Perfect," she exclaimed as I did exactly as she asked. She quickly took a few images on my phone, and then let me get down and get dressed.

She pulled up the viewer and I had to admit she had done a masterful job. The elk was there, the dahlia clear, my abs – even with my ever-increasing love handles – looked fantastic, and there was no way on earth Lucy would know it was me, not even my throat was visible. I dropped a kiss on Callie's forehead.

"You are an absolute star MacAllister."

"Let's just say we're even now shall we? Now get back

to work before you lose your job and let me know how things go!"

I ran back to work, getting back in time to quickly choke down a sandwich and send Lucy the picture. I just hoped she still had enough of her fantastic sense of humor left to take it well and that it hadn't become a casualty of her troubles. She had always been one of those people who could find the best in any situation until her mom had died. I hoped that change had been temporary for her sake.

I struggled through the rest of the day, anxious as to what her reaction would be, making all kinds of mistakes. I handed over the wrong documents at crucial moments, and had to fumble around in piles to find the right ones, and an embarrassing flush seemed to be on my cheeks all through the afternoon session. I breathed a sigh of relief as the judge recessed for the day. I couldn't wait to get home and hear how Lucy had made out with her assessment.

"Cole, everything okay?" Henry Cable the Assistant DA asked me kindly as I was about to head out of the courtroom. "You seem a little on edge today. It isn't like you, you're normally so organized and focused. If there is anything I can help you with?"

My boss was a good man, unusual in an elected official, but this wasn't something I wanted to confide in him: that I was all over the place because of a girl.

"I'm okay sir, just one of those days. I'm a bit tired. This has been a long process." It wasn't an outright lie, I was tired and the case was tough.

"I keep forgetting you're only an intern Cole. You do

your job better than many experienced and fully qualified attorneys. When you graduate next year, don't hesitate to give me a call. If you want a job here you have one, if you want help getting one elsewhere, then if I can pull strings for you I will. You deserve to go far. Anyway, get a good night's rest, I need you sharp tomorrow. Final day can always be tough. But, at least this thing is nearly over now."

"Do you think we have done enough sir?"

"We can only hope so. The jury experts keep telling me we have most of them on our side, but they can do odd things once they get in to vote. It is never over until that verdict is read out. But, between you and me, I am quietly confident. Your work has been a vital part of that. I have never known anyone to write a brief as well as you.
"

"Thank you, I've always wanted to be a public defender. I know there is no glory sir, and certainly very little money, but I've always felt that everybody deserves a fair shot. Too many go down even when they aren't guilty because of a bad defense. I'd like to try and give them a good one where I can, even the bad guys."

"I hope those principles of yours last. You're a pretty earnest type so they probably will. You are sadly all too correct that public interest law doesn't tend to attract the brightest and best. Well, I can certainly put you forward when you pass the bar for that if you are still sure it is what you want then."

"Thank you sir, that means a lot."

I walked away feeling that the day couldn't get more surreal. The Assistant DA himself had taken me aside to tell me he would do whatever he could to smooth my career – after my worst day at the office yet! I hadn't thought he even knew my name, let alone paid attention to the work I had done over the last two summers. With a real spring in my step I raced eager to hear from Lucy and tell her my exciting news.

8

LUCY

I was just showing my tutor Mrs. Braithwaite in as the Trents returned from their vacation. I could feel the nerves build in my stomach, tumbling over one another as if I had a washing machine full of clothes rather than a stomach.

I knew I had delivered my best work yet, but you can never be sure if people will like it. I had slaved so hard to make it exactly what the clients had requested of me, but could honestly say that there was nothing else I could have done to make this elegant colonial style house look any more beautiful.

Yet, with them away for the two weeks I had worked on it I hadn't had any feedback from anyone as to whether I really was heading in the right direction. I nervously gave all three of them the tour, and had then been sent outside to the garden to wait for the verdict. Mrs. Braithwaite had given them a stern warning to give nothing away as they went around the house. They were to make their comments on the forms she gave them, and then the three of them would compare notes at the end. It had been excruciating not being able to gauge their reactions as they all maintained perfect poker faces throughout.

"Lucy, congratulations, it should come as no surprise that you've earned yourself another pass with the highest honors. You are going to have a wonderful career, my dear. Your clients have given you the highest praise in my interview with them. They were surprised by not just the quality of your work, but also that you kept to deadline, within budget, and exactly on the proposal you had discussed," Mrs. Braithwaite said breathlessly as she crossed the perfectly manicured lawn to where I perched on the wicker lounge furniture.

The redoubtable Mrs. B really should have retired years ago. Her perfectly set white curls and her prim floral suits were a bit of a campus joke to those who didn't know her. She also had a reputation for being pretty fierce, demanding, and highly critical. Her nickname, "The Old Dragon," was one I had never understood and I found little about her to laugh at. I've always found her to be a very kind lady, though direct and to the point, and she knows more about interior design than many of the younger and more fashionable designers who taught us will probably ever learn. I loved her right from the start, and had been so glad when her face had appeared around the door at exactly five p.m. to supervise the tour.

I figured that if anyone would give me a fair appraisal it would be her, and she was saying I had crushed it! I could hardly believe my ears and wanted to pick her up and swing her around with happiness, but decided she might not take that too well, so settled for a firm handshake. She shocked me by pulling me into a big bear hug.

"I've had my eye on you since you were an undergraduate. You had promising skills when you came here, thanks to your mom instilling an artistic critical eye in you from an early age, and your dad's excellent woodwork training, but you've grown so much as an artist... your unique approach to work was all your own doing. I am so very proud of you for doing so well. You have never made me change my mind about your abilities. I am certain that the Trents will be telling everyone they know about what a truly stunning job you have done on their house. You will get a lot of work from this Lucy. Would you like me to help you to take some photographs to go in your portfolio?"

"Thank you so much, but no, I'm good," I said beaming, "I've taken a ton already, there's only a few rooms left that I need to do. Then after that, all that's left to do is to gather my things and get out of the way. Thank you again, Mrs. Braithwaite. You have been a fantastic mentor."

"Call on me any time Lucy. Here take my card. I have a feeling this is the beginning of a fantastic career. I want the bragging rights that I helped you on your way!"

She pressed a business card into my hand, and walked calmly back down the garden path to her car. I wanted to dance for joy, but managed to keep it to a quick jig. I ran back up to the house where Margot Trent was pouring out a bottle of perfectly chilled champagne.

"Congratulations Lucy, we absolutely love it. I think you just passed with flying colors right? Time for a little celebration don't you think?" I laughed at her excitement on my behalf.

"Definitely. I'm so pleased that you like it. And how was the vacation?" I asked politely as I took the crystal flute she held out to me and sipped slowly. The bubbles tickled as they went down, but it was crisp and dry and delicious, though I wouldn't want to drink it all the time.

"Dan said it was too hot, I hated the hotel, but the island was stunning!" she chuckled. "It was great Lucy, but I have to say I am so pleased to be home, especially now my home looks like this. I am so sorry I ever doubted you could do this inside two weeks. Wow!"

"I love my den Lucy. You got it exactly right," Dan Trent said warmly as he brought in their suitcases, kissed his wife, and accepted a glass of champagne. He raised his glass. "To the first of many incredible jobs, eh?"

We all clinked our glasses, which rang with a clear note telling me just how expensive they must have been. I tucked a stray strand of my hair back behind my ear a little bashfully.

"Is it okay if I just take a few more pictures?" I asked.

"Sure, and Lucy, if a client ever wants to see what you can do in the flesh so to speak, don't hesitate to give us a call and we can arrange a suitable time for you," Dan said earnestly.

"Gosh, thank you, that is so generous of you both."

"Think nothing of it, and of course we will be telling and showing all our friends. I hope you have made sure we have plenty of business cards to hand out for you. I think we are going to need them!" Margot said enthusiastically.

"Oh, and there's this. No, don't you dare refuse it,"

Dan said as he handed me a thickly stuffed envelope full of fifty-dollar bills. I gasped.

"But I'm not allowed to take payment other than materials for college work," I tried to protest.

"You have worked non-stop for two weeks by the looks of it, your tutor doesn't have to know, and it would have cost us ten times as much if we hired you now. It is the least we can do. You have done an incredible job. You deserve to be rewarded with more than just a piece of paper, Lucy. Thank you so much for making our house a home. It truly is perfect," Dan said warmly.

I moved around the rooms in a slight but contented daze, taking shots from all sorts of angles. I got up on a ladder to get as close to full room shots as I could, and took close-ups of some of the smaller details I had included to personalize each space. I couldn't wait to get home and tell Apollo and Alison all about it. Finally finished, I packed up my camera, and shook the Trent's hands warmly, leaving them to enjoy their new home in peace.

I treated myself to a cab home, and was amazed to see that the envelope contained two thousand bucks! That could keep me comfortably for another three months if I was careful with it. I kissed the envelope and sent a little prayer of thanks to my generous first paying clients. I pulled out my phone to tell Ali the incredible news, to find a message from Apollo waiting for me.

So, how did it go? And what do you think? ;-)

He'd attached a picture as I had asked. I couldn't help but laugh at the shot he had sent, but as my initial reaction died down I took a closer look at the finely cut abs, the muscular but gentle looking hands and the firm pecs that had just the right amount of definition. Apollo was certainly built like the Greek god he'd named himself for, that was for sure. I was surprised to find my body reacting to just a picture, but my breath came a little faster, my nipples grew taut and I felt an aching pull deep within that I hadn't felt in years, since Cole in fact. This guy was sexy, no doubt about it. He was kind, he was funny, and I couldn't deny any longer that I really liked him.

My fingers trembled as I typed the words, but Alison was right. I had to come out my shell sometime. I had to move on.

Okay Apollo. It's time for the full reveal. Do you like Japanese? If you do then meet me at Nom Nom Sushi, Sunday night 8 p.m!

You're on! But you didn't answer my other question?

I was confused, then looked back at the message, trying not to get distracted by his super hot body this time. I laughed as I realized that he had managed to make me forget two weeks, scratch that, two *years* of crazy hard work just by showing me his deliciously tanned man flesh.

Great, I'll tell you all about it on Sunday!

The cab pulled up outside my block and I peeled off a fifty to pay him. It made me laugh out loud to hear a driver ask me for the first time in my life "Haven't you got anything smaller?" and having to answer him in the negative. He grumblingly gave me my change and I grabbed my stuff and raced into the apartment hoping I would catch Alison before she headed off to the theater.

She was sat on the couch biting her nails anxiously.

She turned, her face pale, as she heard me tumble in the door.

"I passed with full honors, I have a date with Apollo, the Trents paid me two thousand bucks, and have you ever seen anything as fucking drop dead sexy as that!" I burst out as I thrust my phone and the picture of Apollo and the elk in front of her.

"Whoa, slow down Luce, I know I don't have much time but seriously, can all that happen in the space of one day?" I nodded, suddenly unable to speak as the reality of it all hit me too. She looked at the picture. "Mmmm, well you wouldn't kick him out of bed for eating crackers that's for sure! Who cares what his face looks like when the rest of him looks that good!"

"Uh-huh," was all I could manage. I thrust the envelope full of bills at her. "Take whatever I owe you Ali, you've paid my share of so much this last month or two."

"No honey, you hang on to that. That is your seed money while you get up and running. You'll need it. You won't get paid on jobs until they are done, so having a month or two worth of backup money will really help you out. You pay me back once you are doing okay."

"Okay," I mumbled, suddenly exhausted. It had been a very big day all around.

"I knew you'd do great. And I can't believe you have a date! Did he ask you?"

I shook my head as a torrent of giggles escaped. "Nope, I asked him."

Her eyes bulged. "Okay, who are you and what have you done with my friend?"

She pulled me into a hug and whispered, "I am so happy for you."

"You'll help me figure out what I can wear for the date, won't you?"

"Try and stop me. But we're going to have to talk about it all tomorrow because I am running late as always. I am going to be so glad when this run is over and we are in rehearsal for the new play. Go take a nap, and we'll celebrate when I get done tonight. I'll bring pizza and champagne unless you'd rather have a night on the town?"

"Pizza and beer would be great. I had champagne already today. It was nice, but not that great I need to do it again. Go break a leg."

She kissed me on the cheek and we headed towards the door together. She squeezed my arm proudly and headed out and I closed the door behind her and headed down the hallway to my room.

Crashing down onto my bed I looked at the picture of Apollo again. He really was such a smart-ass, sending me his body and not his face. I liked his style. I couldn't deny I also liked his perfectly sculpted body too.

Everything in my life seemed to be falling into place for a change and I had things to look forward to. I almost wished that Sunday would get here sooner. I could hardly wait to meet him and see if we really were a good match. I hugged the phone to my chest and fell fast asleep.

9

COLE

"I believe there is a booking in the name of Lucy Rivers, for two?"

The concierge looked me up and down critically. Clearly I passed some kind of test, as he then deigned to check in the book for our reservation.

"Follow me sir," he finally said in a high-pitched voice. I was a little surprised by it; he was quite a large man, built well. But I did as I was told. He showed me to a table, tucked away in an alcove. The restaurant was buzzing, filled with a few intimate couples, a rowdy group or two as well. It was clearly very popular and I loved the brick walls and simple décor throughout. It felt honest and looking at the colorful and aromatic food that was emerging from the kitchen I could see exactly why Lucy had suggested it.

I sat down with my back to the door. I didn't want to scare her away too soon. My stomach was roiling with nerves. I felt like I had swallowed a whole cave full of bats and they wanted out. It was now or never, I thought.

Everything I had hoped for with all those crazy trips up and down the country, to every college and university except, ironically, those in Massachusetts and Rhode Island, and it had all come down to this single night. Would I be able to convince her to stay, to hear me out? Would she see this as yet another manipulation or betrayal? Would she give me the time to explain?

I hadn't told Mom or Tom. I didn't want to get their hopes up and to have it all go wrong again. I hadn't even told Jake or Callie that she'd finally agreed to a date. I wanted her all to myself for just this one night. I wanted to see how it went, without the potential pity or over-excitement that my friends or family might add to it all. I just wanted to see her face, in the flesh, once more.

I tapped at the table with the chopsticks, anxiously drumming as I watched the clock above the kitchen door tick closer to eight p.m. Why had I come so early? Being here fifteen minutes beforehand so I could ensure I wasn't easily spotted before she even got into the restaurant had seemed like such a good idea. Maybe I should have gone with the making her wait, but then she would have been mad at me for being late, as well as everything else.

Fuck, this had been such a stupidly crazy idea.

Finally, after what had felt like an absolute eternity, I heard footsteps behind me.

Instinctively I knew this was it. These footsteps didn't belong to a passing waiter or another customer; no, behind me, in the very same room was my Lucy and my whole body vibrated with anticipation.

"Apollo?" a tentative voice enquired.

I took a deep breath, stood up and turned round.

Lucy looked amazing. She was wearing a cute kimono styled dress, cut so short that it made her fabulous legs look like they went on forever. But all that didn't matter as our eyes met and I took her in.

Her face was as perfect as I remembered it, a tiny smattering of freckles across the bridge of her nose, and that thick, curly auburn hair that made her resemble a wild woman. And then, there were the flashing eyes that had started off so soft and yielding, that were now blazing daggers at me.

"Cole!" she spat, frown lines creasing her now-furious face. Lucy stepped forward and for a second I thought she was about to hug me. But then her arm arced through the air and she slapped me, hard across the cheek.

Whoa, I had not been expecting that, I thought, as I palmed my stinging cheek. I shook my head to try to regain my composure, but I was already too late to put out a hand to try and stop her. She stormed back out through the restaurant as if a tiger were on her tail. I threw a couple of tens on the table and raced after her.

Fuck, fuck, fuck.

I had screwed it up, all over again. I had hurt her, lied to her and why on earth had I ever expected her to sit down calmly and just talk it all out? Stupid, Cole, really stupid idea!

I craned my neck to see her, looking left and right, and finally glimpsed her hightailing it down the street, her cloud of hair bobbing behind her.

"Lucy!" I yelled. She turned to look at me over her shoulder but instantly turned away, running even faster.

I chased after her, realizing pretty suddenly just how unfit a summer in the DA's office had left me, but there was no way I was going to let her go. Not now. I was soon panting trying to keep up with her. She was in great shape, her pert derriere seemed to dance along the street, always just out of reach.

"Lucy, stop. I just want to talk!" She ignored me.

Gritting my teeth I put in a final burst of speed. My thighs burned as I ran and slowly but surely I managed to get level with her.

I grabbed her arm and dragged her into the nearest alleyway. I couldn't say what came over me as I muscled her against her will, kicking and screaming, further in where we wouldn't be seen and used my body weight to pin her up against the wall. I am in no way a violent man, but I had to make her talk to me, had to get her to hear me out.

"Let me go, Cole. Or I'll scream!"

I was frantic, and could see from her eyes just how frightened she was. Coming to my senses I loosened my grip a little, but not enough that she would be able to get away from me.

"Lucy, I don't want to hurt you, I promise. I just need to talk with you, to know you're okay." I pleaded with her, as her vivid green eyes threw nothing but pure hatred my way. I sagged with disappointment at how badly I had screwed everything up. *Again*. I resorted to the absolute truth, hoping it would help her understand why I was being so brutal, acting so completely out of character.

"I love you, you crazy woman."

Lucy stopped squirming as she digested my words and her eyes softened. Seconds passed by as we caught our breath.

God, we were so close and it felt like my every brain

receptor was on overload. I could hardly process that she was here in front of me, my hands touching the bare silky skin of her arms, my torso against hers trapping her. A waft of her sweet vanilla perfume mingled between us, making the bulge between my legs thicken, hardening with desire.

She swallowed. I knew she could feel my cock pressing up against her, but still she wanted to be set free.

"Cole," she sighed. "Let me go."

"No, not until I say what needs to be said." Shit, where to begin, I thought. Now she was here, all the words that I wanted to say were jumbled about. *Just be honest.*

"Do you know how long I've waited for this moment? Fuck, Luce, you know I love you. I have loved you pretty much my entire life. I have searched up and down the entire country trying to find you – as has your dad. We have been worried sick. I get you are mad at me, I tricked you and that was wrong, but would you have ever met with me if you knew who I was?" My voice was choked with passion, and hurt, and the years of pain not knowing where she was had not assuaged.

She shook her head, and her eyes blazed again.

"No Cole, you're right. I wouldn't have come," she said. "But loving me isn't enough to fix what you've done. What on earth happened to you that you could do this to a woman, any woman?"

I had no defense, except the excuse of unyielding love. Yet, she was right, I could hardly believe what I done either.

"God, I have missed all of you so very much, but it isn't enough just to say 'I love you,' and magically everything goes away and is all right," she said.

There were tears pouring down her cheeks, and I could feel them pricking in the back of my own eyes too. I let go of her arm and brushed away the wetness on her face, then cradled my hand along her jawline. Hers was the face I'd fallen head over heels for oh so long ago.

Our eyes locked and her chest rose and fell in rapid succession as my fingers smoothed down and across her bottom lip. One last chance, I thought, a last ditch effort.

And even if I wanted to, I couldn't stop myself. The temptation of being so close, feeling her lithe body pressed up against mine was more than my tortured soul could bear.

I bent my head to hers and claimed her mouth before she could object. It was angry, and full of all the pent-up frustration and rage that we had missed out on so many years, that she was still so damn stubborn, and that no matter how hard I tried I just couldn't get her out of my head.

She didn't respond at first, taking a moment to melt into it. A moan escaped her mouth, and slowly, so very slowly, her hand crept up to the back of my neck, her work-roughened fingers twining in the hair at the nape of my neck. Her lips parted, and finally she kissed me back – as hungry for me as I was for her.

It was nothing like our first one, the sweet kiss of exploration all those years before, the one that had haunted me all these years. No, this was full of adult passion and fury. It was hot as hell, and I could feel my cock pulsing against her taut belly. I lifted her up and she wrapped her legs around my waist, rocking her pelvis against mine in a tortuous rhythm that my body responded to instantly.

"You don't know how many times I've thought about this," I groaned as I found her mouth again.

I held her tightly, never wanting to let her go – but knew that we would have to break this surging, passionate embrace and talk eventually. I just prayed again and again that she would give me a chance to speak, and would hear me out this time.

She felt so good, pressed tightly against my chest, her hands clawing at the muscles of my shoulders and back. Her buttocks were perfect in my hands and I longed to touch and taste her everywhere, to peel her dress away and reveal her body underneath.

"Cole," Lucy gasped as I planted kisses up her exposed neck. "Stop, Cole. We need to talk..."

The spell was broken. This was not the right time, nor the right place, and I tentatively began to withdraw from her. I set her back down tenderly, but still held her close to my heart.

"Okay, let's go back to the restaurant. We can talk there."

She shook her head and started to push me away, her hands upon my chest. "No, Cole. I changed my mind. I can't do this... any of this."

I took a step back from her, trying to understand what she was saying, but my mind was not putting it together. I was too fucking horny, and it was too difficult to think.

"Why the hell not? Come on Luce, I don't claim to know anything about you these days, but the girl I once knew is still in there. That kiss just proved it. Not to mention the all the emails and texts over the last few weeks. That Lucy loved her family, loved her friends, and always gave everyone the benefit of the doubt. She's still in there," I said, not knowing if I was trying to persuade her or convince myself.

"That Lucy died when Steph made my dad betray my mom," she stated blankly, the passionate desire in her eyes replaced by a flat misery that overtook her in an instant.

"I don't believe that, Lucy. Please, can't we go somewhere and talk?"

"Fine, but not the restaurant, anywhere else. And don't expect it to change anything, and don't think you'll be able to get your own way again by using this...this attraction between us."

Her face was sulky and she was grimacing in a way that reminded me so much of the Lucy who had haunted the home we had shared for that final year, the one that had withdrawn and become moody and unrecognizable when she hadn't gotten her own way.

Knowing we needed somewhere neutral to go, I suggested we just go to a small diner we passed. We walked stiffly as far apart as she could manage back down the main street.

A waitress took our order and brought our drinks. Cola for me, and a root beer float for her. It could have been any one of a hundred nights we had sat together in the diner back home. She stared at me, clearly waiting for me to speak. Now I had her here I had absolutely no idea where to start. I was tongue tied again – probably not the best thing for a prospective lawyer. But Lucy and those gorgeous eyes always had a way of making me feel speechless.

"Congratulations on fulfilling your dreams, Lucy," I

began tentatively, knowing that was the dumbest thing I could've said.

"Thank you," she said as primly as an old spinster. It made me laugh. She glared at me. I had to admit though, seeing those perfect eyes so full of fire and passion again, rather than the blank nothingness that had replaced it, had me feeling hot and bothered all over again. I was glad that the booth would hide just by how much.

"Oh come on, Lucy, give me a break here, please? All I did was support my mom, who also had a pretty tough time of it after my dad left if you remember. So I figured she deserved a bit of happiness, so sue me!"

Lucy was staring down at the table, shaking her head.

"This again? Fine, let's get it all out in the open. I know your mom had it tough too, but why couldn't she find someone else. Anyone but my dad?" She sighed heavily.

"I was just so mad at everything. I was mad that my mom was gone, and I was mad that she was taken when the most important part of my life was happening. You know how my grades went to shit – for God's sake you even offered to hack into the school computer to change them for me! I was angry that just as we seemed to be developing a relationship – a real one – that it was snatched away from us. And the worst thing of it all was that it seemed that nobody else missed Mom like I did. How could my dad even be thinking about a relationship with someone else, let alone getting married again and having a god damn baby?! And, that it was *your* mom. Don't you see? It ruined everything between us, made you my brother when I wanted you to be my boyfriend. It was just all so fucking wrong!"

10

LUCY

It was the first time I had let any of that stuff out. I could hardly believe my own ears, as everything I'd been holding back for that last few years seemed to just tumble out of me. Oddly, having finally admitted to it all, I felt lighter.

He didn't seem to be shocked by anything I had said. He had always known me so well and it seemed he still got me better than anyone else ever had, even Alison.

I raised my eyes to look at Cole and instantly remembered our kiss, the one that had made my knees tremble. I bit my lip trying to force myself not to think about it, not right now. I had to hold onto my fury. It was the only thing that had kept me going all these years... and yet, one look at his soft kissable lips was melting my resolve. I wanted him to do it all over again; to touch me, to slip his tongue into my mouth and make those shivers dance like static over my arms again.

"Luce, you have carried all that for all these years. I hated it that you suddenly became my sister too. It sucked having to see your sexy legs everywhere I turned in the house, and the memories of those times I caught you in the shower have been imprinted in my memory ever since, but none of it was like you think it was. Mom and Tom didn't ever betray your mom. Jo wanted them to get together, wanted them to keep our families together, wanted to make sure that two heartbroken people wouldn't be lonely. Yes, they did fall in love too – but your mom was pushing them together before she was even gone."

"Yes, everyone kept trying to tell me when I was sixteen. I remember all the excuses. I know nobody thought I was listening, but seriously, did anyone expect me to believe that crap?" I retorted, angry again.

"My mother would have been mortified to think her husband cared for her so little that he could remarry, and even worse have a child with anyone within a year of her dying. It is sick and twisted, and just too damn convenient to blame the dead woman. No Cole, you won't get me to forgive them. I think maybe I forgave you a long time ago, but I am not even close to being ready for that."

He looked at me sadly, and I knew he felt that I meant that this was goodbye.

Our burgers arrived, and we ate in silence.

Every bite was like sawdust, and I almost choked trying to swallow it down. I just wanted to escape and mourn the loss of my best friend all over again. Not only had I lost Cole all for the second time, but my beloved Apollo, the guy who had made me feel so safe, had given me such hope for the future.

I tried not to think about the kiss, that brutal and bruising clinch we had shared in the alleyway. My body so clearly still wanted him, badly, and I tried to banish thoughts of his wanting manhood pressing hard against me away.

I had never felt such a connection with anyone other than Cole, though I didn't have much to compare it with. I didn't exactly let anyone get close to me anymore. But just sitting near him there was electricity tingling through every cell of my body, and I wanted him, even now.

He suddenly put his burger down, without having taken a bite. "Lucy, I don't know if I can just get up and walk away from you when we finish this meal."

I put my fork down, and took a sip of my root beer. I needed to give myself time to think about what he was saying. I didn't want to walk away from him either, but I couldn't see a way we could ever be together. He was still a part of the family I still wanted nothing to do with.

He was still my stepbrother.

"I don't either, but I can't ask you to turn your back on your mom. I won't. It sucks having no family, and I wouldn't wish it on anyone – but I can't accept them, not yet, maybe not ever."

"Would you maybe be able to accept me if I don't rub it in your face about them, or anything about back home? Could you take just me, no other baggage?"

His eyes pleaded with mine, the deep and melting brown irises so warm and inviting. I didn't want to say no, but didn't know if either of us were making any kind of a realistic decision. His family was such a huge part of him, of who he was. His emails and texts had told me that – even if I hadn't known it about him from all those years of friendship. Could he really be expected to never talk about them with me? Would he even want to?

It was madness and selfish to ask it of him. I shook my head. "Cole, you love them. Steph, Dad, and is it... Morgan? You've talked of virtually nothing else in your emails. I don't think I can ask you to do that, to never mention them around me. It would be unfair and cruel."

"No, I can do it. I can keep it separate."

I shook my head again, trying to stop the tears that were threatening to fall all over again from coming as I saw the desperate look in his eyes, pleading with me.

"Seriously Lucy, I can do it. I have more than enough things in my life I can talk about with you. My work, your work, my studies, music, friends. We can do this. I can't lose you again, I just can't."

I wanted to be selfless, and knew it was the right thing to do. I wanted to make him walk away from me and never come back, but I wanted him too badly to let him go. I knew it would only ever end in heartbreak for us both, all over again, but I needed him. I always had. Stepbrother or not, he was the only guy who had ever made my heart flutter and my body react with such fire. I wasn't strong enough to do what was right.

"You're sure?" I asked tentatively.

He nodded, and grasped my hand tightly as if he never wanted to let it go. I reached up to cup his cheek. I stroked the soft skin, feeling the slight stubble of his beard and looked for the sweet boy I had known. He was still in there, behind all the sharp masculine lines, but the changes on him looked so much better than any man had a right to look.

"Then I think we should get the check and get out of

here, before I let you kiss me again." I said, trying to make a joke.

He didn't need asking twice, and within minutes a cab was dropping us off at his apartment. It was tiny, just a combined kitchen and living room, bathroom, and bedroom. It looked a little shabby, but it was clean and tidy. Cole had always been that way. I smiled; glad to see that hadn't changed. I was the messy one – for all my passion for gorgeous interiors I could turn a clean room into an artistic whirlwind in a matter of minutes.

He had barely shut the door when I flung myself at him. I didn't want any more talk tonight. I just wanted to lose myself in him, and then take each day minute by minute until the inevitable would happen and it would become too difficult. I would let myself have this night with him; there would be no guilt, no thoughts of anyone else. Just me and him... as it was supposed to be.

※

I KISSED HIM FIERCELY, feeling my body react as soon as I touched him and he touched me. Every bit of me was so hypersensitive, and the lightest caress made me quiver with anticipation. He lifted me up and carried me to his bed, laid me down as if I were the most precious treasure in the world. I reached up and pushed the curtain of shiny nut brown hair out of his eyes as he leaned down to kiss me on my already-parted lips. I arched up toward him and our mouths met, more gently this time. This was a kiss of exploration, not domination, and I welcomed his probing tongue. I sucked on it gently and was delighted by a little groan that escaped his throat.

My hand slipped up his hard torso, pushing up his shirt, eager to see in person the beautiful body he had sent me a picture of. I traced every ridge, licked at his nipples and kissed the firm ridges of his abs once he collapsed beside me.

Feeling oddly empowered, I straddled his body, and slowly undid the buttons on my little black dress. I watched his face, and was rewarded as pure lust flashed across his features as I lifted the hem up and over my head.

Starting with his hands on my waist he traced a heavenly line up toward my bra. He slipped his fingers over the material, cupping my breasts, as my nipples strained against the lace of my black and pink bra. He moved the fabric aside, and teased the nipple, leaning up to take it in his mouth. He sucked gently, the tip of his tongue fluttering around my bud, causing me to moan.

I could feel myself getting wetter with his every touch, his every look. My hips strained against his, rubbing at his engorged cock. We both cried out softly from the exquisite torture.

Suddenly he grabbed me by the arms, and rolled me underneath him. He trailed kisses from my lips, down my throat, the cleft between my breasts, moving farther and farther down until he reached the tiny wisp of lace that were my panties. I was almost embarrassed I was so wet for him, but he seemed to delight in having brought me to such a peak of arousal.

"You want me to kiss you there?" he asked, a knowing smile on his face.

I nodded and clutched at the bars of the metal bed frame behind my head as he nibbled and teased at my nipples once more. His hands eased the panties down my legs, and he dipped a finger between my lower lips.

"Oh, god yes."

"You're so beautiful, Lucy. And I'm going to show you how much I've missed you... and how much I love you."

His words sent my clit throbbing, not to mention the way he rubbed at it, gently back and forth then circling it lazily. I gasped and felt my hips pushing up to meet his hand. He dipped his fingers lower, and pushed a finger up inside me, still caressing my clit with his thumb. I was on fire with him inside me, but desperately wanted more.

He kissed me deeply, capturing my tongue, suckling at my bottom lip as a rush of lightning deep within my core ignited as he worked his magical fingers, thrusting hard until I quivered all over from my first release. I could feel the walls of my pussy tightening round his fingers, and the wave of pleasure left me feeling all floaty and light. But he wasn't done with me yet.

He moved to the end of the bed, and pushed my legs wide apart. Gazing for a moment at my exposed center I had the sudden urge to cover myself.

"Don't you dare," he warned as if he knew what I was thinking, and then licked his lips. I felt my cheeks redden. The way he looked at me, at my pussy, as if he wanted to devour me... no one had ever looked at me like that before.

Cole lifted up my buttocks slightly and placed a pillow beneath them. He dipped his head and disappeared from view, his hot breath my only way of knowing where he was. And then suddenly he began to taste and lick, nibble and caress.

He focused all his skill on my tender clit and I almost

cried out from the sheer pleasure. But I simply couldn't stop myself from crying out when he plunged his fingers into my pussy while he continued to lavish his attention on my sensitive nub.

"Oh my God, Cole, stop, please I don't know if I can take anymore!"

He looked up at me, a lascivious look in his eyes.

"Are you sure you want me to stop?" he asked as he kept up the rhythmic thrusts.

"No, yes. Oh I don't know. I want you inside me Cole, I need you inside me!" I cried.

He was more than happy to oblige me. He ripped off his briefs and grabbed a condom from a drawer by the side of the bed. He slipped it on and moved carefully so the tip of his cock was poised right at the entrance to my pussy.

For a fleeting moment I managed to get a glimpse of his engorged cock, so thick and ready. And then it was gone as he plunged himself inside me, obliterating any coherent thoughts I may have had.

I gasped. I had never felt so full.

He eased in, right up to the hilt and bent to kiss me tenderly, his fingers finding and playing with my nipples at the same time. I raised my legs up around his back as my feet pressed gently against his firm butt, and encouraged him to move within me.

Our eyes held and locked and we gazed at each other as the tension built.

With each slap against my rump, as he pushed into me and I pushed towards him, his cock found its way deeper and deeper inside me with every thrust. He pushed my legs up onto his shoulders and I felt him even deeper within, right at my very core. The friction of his pelvis against mine made me cry out over and over again until I was breathless and at his rhythmic mercy.

"I can't hold on any longer Lucy," he rasped throatily, his fingers kneading into the flesh upon my hips.

"I'm nearly there, fuck me harder," I burst out. He increased the grip he had upon me and picked up speed, thrusting within me, the sound of our panting and our skin slapping together echoing around the room as we moaned with abandon.

"Cole, yes. Oh, fuck..."

I began to feel his penis begin to contract within me, and my own internal muscles began a series of spasms that took me headlong into the most overwhelming orgasm of my life.

Lights sparked across my eyes and I clawed at his back, holding on tight, never wanting the feeling to disappear, as my toes curled and my whole body went rigid.

I loosened my grip, leaving little half-moon shaped indents left in his skin. He withdrew tenderly, then we collapsed back onto the bed. He turned to dispose of the condom quickly, then returned to hold me against his chest.

"I'm never letting you go," he whispered from behind me.

I nodded and leaned back against him. I finally felt that I was where I belonged, in the arms of the man I loved, the only man I had ever loved.

I knew it wouldn't last, but I was selfish enough to want to grab what I could get before the real world intruded on us once again. I shivered as I thought of life without him. He gently pulled up the covers, thinking I was cold. I snuggled even tighter into his body, content to lie there in silence until we both drifted off to sleep.

I WOKE up in the morning, and had to pinch myself to check if it had all been real. I gazed sleepily around me at Cole's tidy man cave, and reached out to the other side of the bed. He wasn't there, but it was still warm. He clearly hadn't been gone long. I lazed happily, listening to the sound of him puttering around in the room next door.

He appeared with a tray and a grin, dressed in only his suit trousers. True to his word he didn't mention anything about family, kissed me good morning like he'd been doing it for years, and pulled on a freshly ironed shirt.

"God, you look so hot in my bed," he groaned, "I don't want to go, but I have to get to work. I promise I will call you later, and I want to see you tonight. I have to see you again tonight, no questions asked."

I shuffled my butt up the bed, bringing the covers to my chest as I watched him get dressed. It felt good to be wanted, to be needed. And most of all to have him back in my life.

"And what if I was busy washing my hair?" I teased.

"In that case," he said as he stopped wrapping his tie around his neck and stalked back over to the bed, leaning down close so that I could feel his breath on my neck, "I'm just going to have to lock you up, won't I?"

I shuddered as a thousand tingles tap-danced all over

my bare skin. I'd willingly stay chained to his bed if he continued to talk to me like that, I thought.

"Well, how about I cook you dinner here tonight? You can keep an eye on me as much as you want then," I proposed as he took my breath away and kissed me thoroughly. His lips left mine and I felt a sudden loss; if only we could stay in bed forever and forget about the whole world, shut it all out and catch upon the years we'd lost by being apart.

"Sounds perfect." He slipped his hand under the covers to find my own, grazing my naked wanting flesh as he went, then placed a cool metal object into my palm. "So you can lock up after you, and so you can be here whenever you want."

I grinned while holding on tight to the key. I knew, in the normal world, him giving me the key to his apartment, after just one night, would send most women screaming in the other direction. But this was not just any guy; this was Cole. It felt like we were making up for lost time. All those years we could've had together, I thought wistfully, and it was my fault. The ball of guilt trying to hide in the pit of my stomach told me so.

"Luce, you okay?"

"I'm fine," I replied as I told myself to stop lingering on the past. "Go do some good. I'll be here waiting for you, later."

"Okay, then. I'll see you tonight... I already miss you," he said as he reluctantly tore himself from my arms and headed out of the door.

I stretched languorously then drank the tea and ate the toast he'd brought me, slathered in peanut butter just the way I liked it. I looked around. I hadn't had much time to really take in my surroundings the night before. There had been much more pressing things on my mind. The apartment was cozy, and he had done the best he could with it. I wondered if Steph had given him a hand picking out things, but then scolded myself for breaking my own taboos. *Don't think about them...*

I got up, and showered slowly. The water was warm, and my much loved body felt a little sore in places, but each little twinge brought back a perfect memory. I got dressed and towel dried my hair quickly and was just on my way out back home, locking Cole's door, when my phone rang.

"Hello?"

"Hi, is that Lucy Rivers?" a smooth voice with a hint of Californian twang asked politely.

"Yes, yes it is. How can I help you?"

I didn't know anyone from California, and I just prayed it wasn't someone collecting for my credit card debts. I was a little late in making the payments, but with my windfall it was on my to-do list at the bank this morning.

"Well, a friend of mine told me that you are an incredible interior designer, and I have an entire office building that is in desperate need of some tender loving care. Would you be able to give me a quote on a few rooms - maybe today if you aren't busy?"

"Sure, um, of course." My mind was in overdrive, preoccupied, as I nearly bumped into a pedestrian on the street outside Cole's place. The Trents certainly hadn't wasted any time in telling their friends I was available. I sent up a little prayer of thanks to them. "Sorry, where are you?"

"I run Glitch, we're at the Exchange. You know the big old Victorian block?"

Oh my god! Keep calm and don't say anything stupid!

"Yes! I do! It has been my dream to renovate that place since I moved here. I have been trying to get a meeting with the owners since you bought it!" I said breathlessly. I slammed my eyes shut in regret, I was being too eager, and at this rate I was going to drive her away, I thought. Thankfully my worries were soon soothed.

"Well, with that kind of passion I can see you will fit in well here. Bring yourself and your portfolio over so we can swap ideas. What time can you get here?"

"I could be with you in an hour?" I asked tentatively. It would give me time to get home and get my things and still get there without feeling under pressure – just.

"I have a meeting. It may go on until about twelve, how about we say twelve-thirty?"

"Perfect," I agreed. She hung up and I realized I hadn't even asked her name. Oh well, a quick internet search should sort that out pretty easily.

Standing in the middle of the busy street I wanted to twirl and shout out to the world. I had just had my first client via recommendation. Damn, it felt good!

I raced back to the flat and pulled out all my best pictures, making quick copies of everything. My full portfolio was still at college being graded, but I had duplicates of everything. I grabbed a binder and began to insert pages, showing my progress and finishing with the shots of the Trent's Colonial. Considering it was a rush job, it looked okay.

I picked up my laser measure and my tape measure, thrust them in my coat pockets, and quickly pulled on my interview suit. Glitch always looked like it was a pretty casual place, but I was a big believer in first impressions. I wanted to appear businesslike, someone they could trust with their beautiful building.

I arrived five minutes early, and was told by the bubbly receptionist that Miss MacAllister was still in her meeting. Rather than waste time, I began to look around, taking in the crown molding and chandelier medallions, the stripped-bare fireplaces and the tacky plywood reception desk. I pulled out my sketchpad and began to draw. I was utterly engrossed in my work when I saw a pair of neat black ballet pumps coming my way.

I looked up, and I do mean up, into the smiling face of a six-foot-tall Marilyn Monroe look-alike. She was intimidatingly gorgeous.

"Hello, Lucy?"

I giggled like a nervous idiot; this woman had me right on edge instantly. She was smart, gorgeous, and hyper successful. So much for my good first impression! I put my mechanical pencil down and stood up to shake her hand. "Yes, hi, sorry, you must be Callie MacAllister."

"Pleased to meet you. I have heard great things, and by the look of your sketchbook, all of them are true. I only saw that upside down, do you mind?" She indicated the sketch and I handed it to her. She was either very politely glossing over the fact I had just laughed in her face, or hadn't even noticed it. I prayed it was the latter as she seemed utterly bowled over by the sketch I had been working on. "Wow, you really get this building. Do you really think you could deliver this for us?"

"Sure, it wouldn't be cheap but you can deliver pretty much anything if money is no problem," I joked.

I scolded myself as soon as the words were out of my mouth. I was blowing it, but god she was intimidating. *Pull yourself together! This woman could make your career!*

"Well, money is no problem. Why don't we have a little look around? I don't expect sketches straight off, but just talk off the top of your head to me as we go. Tell me what you see."

I liked her a lot. Sure, she was super hot, and made me edgy as hell – but she was forthright and clearly excited by the prospect of making her workplace beautiful.

We moved slowly. I would spend a few minutes just getting a feel for each space. She didn't jabber and try to fill the silence. I found that very refreshing. She just let me think, let me create. The combination of her peaceful aura and enthusiasm helped me to relax, and I got more and more confident.

I suggested types of furniture, mixtures of traditional and modern fixings to create a fusion of the old building and the new technology the company was all about. I proposed colors and floor coverings, and where rooms could be expanded, or where they should be returned to their original sizes. The building had seen so many changes over the years, but none of them matched or fitted with anything else. It had left a hodgepodge of vacant, functionless rooms with no real identity.

When we reached her office, she pointed toward a big leather swivel chair, and I sat down.

She pulled up a giant beanbag beside me. "So, how long before you can get me sketches for everything, and how much – ballpark – do you think this will cost?"

"The whole thing?" My eyes must've been bulging.

"Sure!"

"Well, the hallway alone would probably take me three days to get sketches and estimates done, and then a few days if you wanted any changes, so say a month for each floor? To do it, you're looking two to three months more per floor. Ballpark figure for my labor, and the painters and contractors I would need to hire, you would be talking a minimum of $50,000 a month plus whatever the materials cost. Fittings, fixtures, and finishes could be anywhere from bargain basement to, well, the sky's the limit depending on how expensive your tastes are."

She nodded and chortled. "Depending on my mood I can be quite extravagant. So, let me see, we are talking anywhere from six figures and upwards, over maybe one or two years?"

"Sounds more than probable." I could only marvel at how nonchalantly she could discuss such a vast sum of money.

"Okay. Let's start with the foyer."

"Right now? Are you serious?" I shook my head. "Sorry, I didn't mean to be rude, I'm just flabbergasted. This has all come out of the blue..."

"That's okay, I totally understand. When I, I mean *we* got our first break setting up our company, we were the same. But yes, I'd want you to start right away. I've left it too long already and this building deserves more than my attempts at decoration," she said as she poked the beanbag beneath her. "Would that be a problem?"

"Oh, no. I'm free as a bird," I said almost singing with joy.

"Good. I'll give you an advance of $5,000 now so you can draw up the sketches, and source contractors and materials. If you let me know if you prefer to deal with payroll for your contractors and yourself, or want me to do it, then we can arrange for that. Do a good job on this, and the rest of the building is all yours, Lucy."

I was trying so hard to keep cool and under control but this was so massively exciting. I loved this building and if I did a good job on the easiest part of it, I would get to renovate and do the entire thing. Dollar signs were flashing before my eyes, and the idea that my first fully professional job would be for such a high-profile company and would take at least a year was utterly unbelievable.

"I'll take some measurements now, if that's okay, and I'll get those sketches over to you right away. I'll also need to arrange a meeting with you so we can talk colors, swatches, and all things decoration."

"Great! Just ask Lesley at the desk to set us up for something by the end of the week if that works for you. I think I have a slot on Friday afternoon."

"Thank you so much, Miss MacAllister," I said genuinely and stuck out my hand again.

"Not at all, and call me Callie," she said as we shook hands. "I'll leave you to do the measuring and I'll get back to work. I'm sure there are some fires that need to be put out."

After taking my time in the hallway, getting the measurements, and making the appointment with the receptionist, I still felt like I was caught in a whirlwind once I finally walked out of the building. I looked back up at the five floors that would soon be my domain in disbelief and actually skipped down the road to the bus stop.

11

COLE

"Thanks so much Callie, Lucy was bouncing all over the place when she called to tell me the news," I said with a huge grin on my face. Finally it felt like I'd done something right and things were going both mine and Lucy's way.

"Hey, I think you may have sent an absolute gem my way Kent, no thanks needed. Did she tell you that in fifteen minutes, she completely redesigned the foyer, sketched what she wanted to do with it freehand, and it was absolutely breathtaking. She is an absolute genius. I have a feeling that I am getting a bargain if I grab her now. That girl is going places. Have you seen her portfolio? Insane doesn't come close to covering it! The building is going to look amazing."

"Well, thanks for even giving her a meeting. This has been what she's always wanted to do, and to hear her talk about your building, well, it's infectious! Anyway, I also called to tell you I'm not going to be able to make drinks as usual on Thursday, though I'm sure that you and Jake will fill the time somehow without me."

"Too right," she said with a snort, but added quickly, "but we'll miss you."

"I have to go home for Mom's birthday party. Don't know how I'm going to get around it with Luce, but I'm hoping that she is going to be so busy with your pitch that she will barely even notice me being gone. Remember, I did not mention her to you – her clients the Trents did. I don't need the hassle right now that would come out of her thinking I had set this up."

"My lips are sealed sugar, but you know I think the both of you are crazy. There is just too much history between you two, to try and live in a bubble. Be careful Cole."

The grin that had been there only moments ago started to whither and die on my face. "I know, I know. I will be, but it's worth it, Callie. She's totally worth it, even if does only last a few weeks."

Fuck, weeks? I wanted it to last for years...

I hung up the phone, and threw myself back into my work. I knew my friends were only being cautious about my relationship with Lucy because they loved me and didn't want me to get hurt, but I wanted them to be as happy for me as I was for the two of them. I groaned. Why did everything have to be so complicated? And I didn't have time to think about any of it now. I had a mountain of paperwork to get done so I could take the afternoon off on Thursday, to guarantee I got down to Newton on time.

I was still trying to decide whether or not to tell Mom and Tom about finding Lucy, but knew they would want to come up here straight away and my perfect bubble would be burst all over again. I would mull it over, and leave it until I got down there to decide. Tom did after all have a right to know she was okay.

MY DAY WAS crazy as usual, but I had never been more glad to be heading home. Lucy would be waiting for me, and we could spend a night together celebrating her new job, and just enjoy being together at last.

She said she was going to cook for me, and I'd promised to bring home a bottle of wine. It felt like we were already an old married couple, and I grinned at the thought – I couldn't think of anything more perfect after waiting so long to have her, let alone see her again. I'd left her a key so she could lock up after herself when she went out this morning, and told her to hang onto it. I liked knowing that she could come and go whenever she wanted, like we were just a normal couple without any past baggage hanging over our heads to worry about.

I thought back to the morning. She'd looked adorable, all curled up in the covers, her mane of hair in tousled disarray like a halo round her lovely face. I hadn't wanted to wake her up, but didn't want to just run out of the house and have her think I was just another asshole who would treat her badly. I had made her breakfast to ease the pain of being roused and she had emerged from the blankets when I took it in. She had seemed really happy. It was so perfect getting to kiss her goodbye and to say that I would see her later on. It was a dream that I wished could go on forever.

I picked up a bottle of a Californian rose that Callie had recommended. I wasn't much of a wine drinker, but if Lucy was going to the trouble of cooking a fancy meal, we should at least have a fancy wine. I also grabbed a box of Belgian chocolate seashells. Lucy had always adored them when we were kids, and had hated flowers. I hoped her tastes hadn't changed too much as I ran up the stairs and opened the door.

"Honey, I'm home," I called out in jest. And though I knew we were in the insanely early stages of our new relationship, the words rang true. Coming home to Lucy would forever be the highlight of my days. "Holy shit! Am I in the right apartment?" I asked in shock as I looked around.

My apartment had been completely transformed. Lucy had worked her magic; it was filled with tiny flickering candles, and a small table and chairs were set up with a perfect white tablecloth, some fabulously expensive looking wine glasses, and a set of heavy cutlery that certainly hadn't come from my cupboards.

"Of course you are, silly," Lucy said, giggling from the kitchen. She appeared with creased napkins, dressed in a delicate summer dress that made her look dreamy and young. "I found pretty much everything from a thrift shop on the way back from Glitch this afternoon. Aren't they fantastic? I saw them and just thought they would all be perfect for here."

"You bought all these for me?" I was really touched. They were such lovely items, and they really did fit in the apartment perfectly.

"The table, and chairs, and everything!"

"You're amazing… come here," I said and reached for her.

"How was your day?"

"Hell, let's not talk about it."

She drifted toward me, and I took her in my arms. The jolt of pure desire I always got whenever I was anywhere near her shot through me, and I wondered if it would ever disappear. I hoped not. She stood up on tiptoe and kissed me warmly.

"Welcome home Cole."

I kissed her back, and would have been more than happy to forget dinner, forget the wine, and just whisk her off to bed there and then. But the buzzer on the oven interrupted us and she unwrapped herself from my embrace and moved swiftly to the small kitchen area where she pulled on oven mitts and bent down provocatively to remove her handiwork.

My cock responded in exactly the way I think she had intended, springing to life at the sight of her pert ass wiggling at me from across the room. She brought the dish over to the table, revealing a perfect Beef Wellington, my absolute favorite dish. When we were kids it had been the dinner my Mom always made on birthdays as an extra special treat.

"I already said you were amazing, didn't I?" I said, feasting my eyes upon the meal before us.

I opened the wine, and presented her with the chocolates. She grinned. "So we both wanted to prove how much we remembered about each other then!"

"Looks like it. Question is, are we both still right? This is still my favorite, and if you have made brownies for dessert then I am putty in your hands!"

"Yup, these are still my favorites, and you got the tea and toast exactly right this morning. Maybe neither of us has changed that much at all."

I kissed her, so glad I finally had the chance to do so whenever I liked. The meal was delicious, and it was fun remembering some of the wonderful moments we had enjoyed as kids. We were both careful not to mention anything that involved anyone else, but it was good to know we had more than enough memories to be able to do so.

She rhapsodized about her new boss, and I had to try really hard not to reveal that I completely agreed with her. Callie really was someone very special. But I decided to just not say anything just yet and instead I told her all about what I was doing in my final week at the DA's office. It would be back to the grind at law school in just ten days, and I wasn't looking forward to it. Too many alumni talked about how tough the final year was, and I knew I was going to have to work harder than ever before.

"Are you going home on Thursday?" Lucy suddenly asked, completely out of the blue.

My mouth dropped open and I stammered to think of anything to say.

"I didn't forget when any of your birthdays were Cole, no need to look so surprised."

"I wasn't.... okay I wasn't expecting you to just blurt it out like that. I thought we weren't talking about them after all."

"I think we both know how unrealistic that is. I don't want make you feel you have to either avoid topics or even worse, lie to me, just so you don't tell me if you are going home for things."

I leaned across the table and took her chin in my hand, and gently pulled her toward me for a kiss.

"Thank you," I said with feeling.

It meant a lot to me that she was thinking of my needs, but even more that my loving Lucy was still there, even if she was still too angry to deal with everything. It did at least give me hope for the future. I couldn't help but want my family to be back together one day. I wouldn't push it, but Lucy seemed to be heading that way on her own.

Lucy reached for my hand and laced her fingers in between mine.

"I don't want to make any of this any more difficult than it has to be for us, Cole. But we need our second chance. I know we have something special, and I promise I won't ever make you feel bad for spending time with them. You love them, and you need them."

She looked unspeakably sad as she said it, and I moved to her side. I took her in my arms, and held her tightly. She loved and needed them too, I thought. I just hoped she would realize it soon for her own sake.

THE PARTY WAS GREAT, and Mom enjoyed herself a lot. I decided not to tell them about finding Lucy until just before I went back to Providence. I wasn't looking forward to it if the lead weight in my stomach was any indication, but felt it was only fair that they know I had found her. Tom still looked so haunted and I knew it would help him to put his mind at rest a little at least.

"Cole, will you read my story tonight?" Morgan asked

sweetly, coming down the stairs in her onesie pajamas, her thumb in her mouth. She only ever did that when she was really sleepy. Mom tried so hard to stop her, but I thought it was kind of cute.

"Sure kiddo, shall we read The Cat in the Hat, or Cinderella?"

I picked her up, and headed up the stairs to her room, glad for the chance to put off my big reveal a little longer. Mom had painted murals of castles, clouds, rainbows, and unicorns everywhere. It was every little girl's dream.

"Cinderella please," she said as she curled up against her pillows. I grabbed the book from the shelf and snuggled up next to her. I began to read. "You have to do the voices Cole!" she exclaimed when I failed to enact the silly voices I usually used for the evil stepmother and ugly sisters.

I did as I was told, and by the time I finished the story, she was fast asleep. I tucked the covers up around her, kissed her on the forehead, turned out the light and left the room. The story had made me wonder how Morgan would take to having a sister. Would she maybe see Lucy as an interloper, trying to take all our love away from her? I hoped not. I really hoped that one day they would meet, and maybe even become friends.

I went back down to the dining room where Mom and Tom were enjoying a last glass of wine together. I took a breath trying to gather as much courage as I would need for the conversation I was about to have.

"Hey guys, I have some news. I'm sorry I didn't say anything sooner, but I didn't want to push anything, or... I don't know."

"Son, you can always tell us anything," Tom said warmly.

"Whatever your reasons for not telling us will have been good ones. We don't need to know what they were if you can't explain," Mom added.

"I've found Lucy," I blurted out.

There was immediate silence, except for the distant ticking of the hallway clock. Both of them looked completely stunned.

"She was in Providence the whole time," I continued, hoping they'd say something sooner rather than later!

"My god, probably the only place we never looked!" Tom exclaimed. "How is she? When can I see her? What is she doing? Is she okay?" he demanded.

"Slow down, Tom, one question at a time. She's fine. She went to Rhode Island School of Design, managed to graduate from their undergraduate program and has just finished her graduate degree in interior design. She is a little bit too skinny, and I think making ends meet has been tough from time to time, but she is okay. She is feisty and crazy and absolutely still our Lucy."

Tom slumped in his chair, tears pouring down his face. "My baby is okay, thank god she's okay," he kept mumbling over and over.

I didn't want to give him false hope so I carried on. "She hasn't forgiven anyone, I'm afraid. She's still mad as hell about everything, but I have managed to get her to speak with me, to even spend time with me. You both know I love her, no shock to anybody there - and I am pretty certain she loves me too but everything is all on the basis that we don't talk about the past."

"Oh honey, that has to be so tough on you both,"

Mom said as she moved to put her arms around Tom and comfort him in his shock.

"It is, but I don't think she is that far from letting us all back in. There have been hints, I don't know, but that maybe in time she may even come home to see you all. I know this will be really hard for you to do Tom, but I think we need to give her the space she needs to do it herself."

Tom nodded, clearly heartbroken that his beloved daughter still didn't want him in her life, but he was a patient man. He would wait. He would trust me and her to work it out. I patted him gently on the shoulder, wanted him to know I could understand that it must be so hard knowing I had seen her, was still seeing her and he could not.

"I think I may have something that just might help, if you really think she is getting closer to forgiving us," Mom said quietly. "I was clearing out some of Joanna's things a few weeks ago in the attic, from her old bureau. I found a letter. It was addressed to Lucy. It's all about what she asked Tom and I to do. I don't know if she changed her mind about giving it to her, or if she meant for me to find it and give it to her before now... but if you think it could help I'll give it to you. It belongs to her. She should have it."

She moved to the sideboard, and pulled a faded crumpled envelope out of one of the drawers.

"I'll give it to her Mom. This may be just what she needs to hear."

Mom gave me a quick squeeze then headed back to Tom's side. He seemed to have gone into shock, and was still murmuring over and over.

"I'll get him to bed, it has been a long day, but thank you for telling us. It is wonderful to know she is safe." Tom nodded his agreement to my mom's words.

I DROVE BACK EARLY the next morning, and headed straight to the office. I could feel the weight of the envelope in my pocket, heavy with promise, and wondered when to give it to Lucy. It could be the key to bringing us all back together, to make everything relatively normal again. But handing it over to her I knew it would not be an easy moment, and I hoped it wouldn't make everything worse.

I had barely been in the office ten minutes when the phone rang. "Cole, it's Mom."

"Hey Mom, what's up? You sound terrible."

"Tom had a heart attack just after you left, we're at the hospital," she said, her voice laden with emotion.

"Is he okay? Is there anything I can do?"

"The doctors are running tests at the moment, so we won't know for sure how bad it was until later. I know you have to work and you wanted to spend the weekend in the city, but I really need you to come home as soon as you can to take care of Morgan. I need to be here with Tom, and Ellie next door can only keep an eye on her today for me. They're going on vacation tomorrow."

I kneaded my forehead. "Shit, you don't think it was because of what I said? About finding Lucy?"

"Oh honey, no. I think it would have happened some time anyway. He has been so anxious and worked up ever since she left home. I know that finding out she was okay was the best thing that has happened to him in years. It is just one of those things. I don't know if you want to tell Lucy, but I think she deserves to know."

"You're right. I don't know how on earth to tell her, but I'll find a way. I'll have to bring Morgan here. I have some final meetings and things I just can't get out of, but I know Callie will be more than happy to take care of Morgan while I'm busy. She adores her."

"Thanks sweetie. I'll see you tonight."

"Take care Mom, and tell Tom I said hi, and to get well soon. We all need him."

I let out a massive sigh as I hung up. Fuck! I couldn't help but feel guilty that my news had somehow caused his heart attack, even though I knew that was impossible. My news, as Mom had said, had probably been everything he needed to hear. But how on earth could I tell his estranged daughter what had happened? And how the fuck was I going to be able to keep everything to do with Mom and Tom out of our relationship when our half-sister would be staying in my apartment for who knew how long?

Our bubble was finally popping after only a couple of days of being together; it was like the world was sending us a sign. I wanted to scream at the top of my lungs for putting obstacle after obstacle in our path. But I was determined to hold onto her no matter what.

I quickly called Callie to check if she would be okay to keep an eye on Morgan for me while I did the things I knew I would not be able to change.

"I am more than happy to help out sugar, but I have Lucy here at the office a lot over the weekend, measuring and doing sketches. Chances are they are going to meet – whether you want them to or not."

"Callie, it is a risk I am going to have to take. I have to take care of Morgan, and I have to get to these meetings. I don't even know if Lucy is going to be talking to me again when I tell her about this, so I can't even think about that right now."

"Good luck sweetie, just drop Morgan off with me whenever you need."

"You are an angel. Thank you, and sorry if any of this puts you in an awkward position. I have a feeling the shit is going to hit the fan, and my blissful bubble is going to burst big time."

"Give Tom our love. I'll send a card and flowers to your Mom."

My day in the office dragged as I got more and more concerned about having to tell Lucy and get back to Newton in time to pick up Morgan from Ellie's. I didn't have time to deal with what was bound to explode. I went straight to Lucy's apartment on my way home, determined to get on my way as quickly as I could.

"Hi, you must be Cole?" A cheerful young woman greeted me at the doorway.

"You must be Alison," I responded politely. "I really need to see Lucy, urgently. Is she in?"

"Hold your horses, you only saw her yesterday. That's love for you," she started, then suddenly stopped, looking carefully at my face. "Shit, something terrible has happened hasn't it?" God I am so sorry, me and my big feet." I looked down at her tiny shoes and managed the first smile since my Mom's call. "I'll just get her. Should I stick around?"

"She may need you, and I have to get going quick, so yes I'd stick around." I was glad she had such a good friend, someone to help her with whatever reaction this news was going to bring.

"Hey Cole," Lucy said as entered the room, moving toward me, her face glowing with happiness. I kissed her fervently, but then pushed her gently towards the couch. "What's up?"

"Lucy, I hate to be the person to tell you this, but it's your Dad. Tom's..." she didn't let me finish. Her mind jumped straight to the worst conclusions. Her face blanched deathly white.

"No, Cole, don't say it. Please don't say he's dead. He can't be dead!" Tears were flooding down her face. I had known all along that she still loved us all, that the anger would not protect her if she found out something terrible. I cradled her in my arms.

"No, he's not dead. He had a heart attack. I don't know how bad it is yet. I'm waiting for Mom to call and update me. I promise I'll let you know as soon as there is any news. But I have to go home. I won't push you to make a decision to come with me, but you deserved to know."

She sobbed in my arms and I held her tightly. She gazed up at me, with abject fear written all over her face.

"I have to take care of Morgan for Mom. She'll be staying with me this weekend. I know you don't want to meet her, so I'll keep her out of your way, but if you need me I will be back in town tomorrow. I have some things I just can't get out of. A friend is going to take care of her while I do what I have to."

Lucy took a cleansing breath and nodded as she wiped away the still streaming tears from her freckled face. "I know I should say none of it matters anymore, that this changes everything, Cole – but it doesn't. Of course, I don't want anyone to die, and I do love them both, but I'm just not ready yet. I can't do it."

"It's okay Luce. I understand. We all understand."

I kissed her on her forehead and Alison passed her a box of Kleenex. She blew her nose loudly, and hiccupped.

"I have to get going, but there was something else." I pulled the envelope out of my suit pocket and handed it to her. "Mom found this a few weeks ago. Maybe it might have some answers for you."

She took it, and just stared at her Mom's handwriting on the envelope. I stood up and moved toward the door. Alison followed me.

"I'll take care of her, keep us updated won't you? Thank god the run has ended and I am around all weekend!"

"Take care of her. I love her so much."

"I will, and I'll make sure she knows."

12

LUCY

I stared at the crumpled letter, hardly daring to open it and see what on earth was inside.

It was hard to believe that just a few weeks ago I had been living in denial of my past and had no thoughts – or very few at least – about my family and was getting on with my life. Things had been going exactly to plan. Now, here I was in love with my childhood sweetheart – there was no denying that fact –my Dad was in hospital, and there was a letter from my dead Mom in my hands. I didn't know what to do with myself, what to think, how to act. Part of me wanted to run after Cole and get in the car and go straight to my Dad's side. The rest wanted me to put my head right back in the sand and pretend I hadn't heard anything about any of it at all.

"Here, drink this," Ali said as she thrust a mug of steaming hot chocolate at me. I took a sip and choked on the huge amount of brandy she had poured into it. "You don't have to work it all out right away," she reminded me. "This is all too huge, so just work through it in waves."

"I can't think about any of it right now, Ali. It is all just too much to even try and comprehend. I think I just need to work. I'll sketch and do some mood boards for Glitch. Callie liked a lot of what I suggested today, so I need to do it while it is fresh. It will help me not to fret about all this. I can't... I just can't think about any of it."

She nodded and rubbed my back.

"Probably a good idea. Want me to answer the phone if Cole calls?"

I nodded and handed her my phone.

"I need to just get lost in something for a while. I'll face up to it, just not now."

I put the envelope down, and moved to my drafting table. I began to work, and quickly the simple acts of cutting and pasting, and drawing and coloring helped me to regain some equilibrium. I barely even noticed Alison turn the TV on to watch a movie. The work was methodical, and it helped me to sort out the jumble in my head.

I loved my dad. I loved Steph. I loved Cole. I loved my mom. But I was still so angry with all of them. Even my Dad almost dying wasn't enough for me to forgive him unconditionally. God, why couldn't I just let it go? Why was I so angry, and who was I really angry with? I simply didn't know anymore.

I put down my tools and moved to the couch. I paced around the coffee table before I finally picked up the letter.

Would Mom have the answers, like she always used

to? *Fuck it,* I thought, *this day couldn't get any worse, can it?* I opened the envelope and pulled out a wad of her favorite floral notepaper. I smiled at the memory of her picking it out in the stationery store.

Her words were simple, and her beautiful handwriting led me onward, tears dripping onto the page with every word. Everything everyone had ever told me was true. I'd been a stubborn fool.

She'd truly wanted Dad and Steph to get married, to build a life together. She hated that she had to leave me, that she wouldn't see me grow up and get married. She knew just how hard it was going to be for me, learning to cope without her. And of course, she wanted me to be happy.

I think the most surprising thing was that my mom knew how I felt about Cole even before I did. The final line made me smile through the sadness.

"My darling girl," it read, "you've got to learn to trust that stubborn heart of yours. If you love each other, and even if he does end up being your stepbrother, then follow your heart like you should and do what makes you both happy."

I wished I had gotten her letter sooner, but then again I probably wouldn't have been ready to hear any of it before now.

Ali had moved to my side, and put her arms around me. She held me like that for what might have been a few moments, and may have been hours. I sobbed, I railed, I was silent, I ranted.

I realized that I had not been angry with anyone really but my mom.

My mom who had left me and never even said goodbye.

I had been so angry that she had said all of this stuff to everyone else, and left me out, trying to spare my feelings. But I knew now she had left me the most personal of goodbyes and I would treasure it always. I knew they were all telling me the truth, had all along. I just hated it that she hadn't told me. That I'd been the last to know. Even now I was fuming that she had left this letter in a place that hadn't been found until now. I missed her so much.

Ali finally put me to bed, her arms curled up around me. I slept like a baby. It was the best night's sleep I think I had ever had, since I had left home at least.

When I woke I knew what I had to do. "I'm going to go home, going to go and see my dad," I told Ali decisively. She grinned at me and hugged me tightly.

"Good for you."

※

I stopped at Glitch to drop off the boards and sketches I'd completed. Even I had to admit they were excellent. Callie welcomed me into the office warmly. "Wow, I love this. When can you start?"

"Well, I'm not sure. I have just had some news that my dad is sick, and so I'm going to go home and make sure he is okay. Can I call you when I know? I know you want to get started as soon as possible, but I really need to go home." She looked at me, and I thought I could see a touch of surprise first off, rather than the clearly genuine concern that followed it.

"Sugar, that is fine. Our daddies are too important to us girls. You take all the time you need. We've waited this long to get started, I doubt if any of us will notice a delay."

"Thanks Callie. I'll be in touch."

I walked down the stairs, and was just crossing the foyer when I saw Cole, walking in through the rotating doors with a tiny redhead at his side. This could only be Morgan, but why on earth would they be here? I panicked, and not feeling ready to meet her yet I ducked behind a load of big boards advertising "Wooed and Won." Thankfully all Cole's attention had been on his, *our* half-sister, so they hadn't noticed my crazed dash for cover. I peeked around the side of the boards and watched as he picked her up onto his shoulders, and walked confidently across the foyer.

"Hey Cole," I frowned as I heard the receptionist say. "And hey Morgan. How are you today, gorgeous?"

Clearly they knew each other well, if she'd met Morgan too. I felt a huge surge of jealousy overtake me, and wanted desperately to be anywhere other than here.

"Hi Lesley, is Callie free? She's going to watch Morgan for me for a bit."

"I think she has just finished with her morning meeting with the interior decorator, but I'll check if it's okay for you both to go up."

I watched as Cole bent down to tie the laces on Morgan's tiny pink sneakers. He tweaked her on the nose and she grinned up at him.

"Will you take me for ice cream later?" she asked him.

She clearly adored him, but absolutely had him wrapped around her cute little finger. I couldn't help but think that he would maybe make a great dad one day, if his patience with her was anything to go by.

"Sure kiddo, whatever flavor you want. As long as you are a really good girl for Callie."

"Callie lets me braid her hair, and always gives me loads of paper to draw with. I'll be good for her."

I could hardly believe my ears. Not only did Cole and Morgan know Lesley, but they were clearly on very intimate terms with Callie, my new boss. Suddenly fuming once more, I wanted to storm out and confront him about all sorts of things: for using my feelings for him to try and get me to go back home, manipulating my life so he could feel less guilty about it, getting me this job for his girlfriend so he could get off letting me down again scot-free.

But now wasn't the time. However I had gotten the job, I needed it. I would not ruin my reputation for being professional because of a two-timing guy like Cole Kent. And, I would still go home to be with my dad, because he and Steph needed me, and my mom wanted me to be a part of their family. I had spent long enough avoiding all of them. Keeping out of the way of just one would be easy as pie, but I wouldn't let him ruin my chance at reconciliation with my father.

I waited for him to head up the stairs, but Callie had chosen to come down. I was forced to watch as Cole embraced her and kissed her. "Thanks for helping me out. Can't tell you how much it means to me," he said.

"Sugar, me and Morgan always have a great time together, don't we sweetpea?" Morgan nodded happily up at the human-sized Barbie doll she was about to get to play with. "Anything for you. I owe you big time after these last few weeks!"

The last few weeks?! What on earth had he done for her to make her so fawningly grateful to him? How had he had the time, or the stamina to be with us both? I put my fingers in my ears, not wanting to hear anymore, and waited until I was sure he was gone. I peeked out to make sure the foyer was empty. Even Lesley seemed to have vanished, and I ran out of the building as fast as I could toward the bus station.

THE HOSPITAL WAS clean and everywhere was glaringly bright. I have never much liked fluorescent lighting. It gives me headaches. But I moved through the corridors as quickly as I could. I was so scared that I would lose my nerve, and run straight back out of there. My dad was out of ICU and was on the cardio-thoracic ward. I could only hope that was a good thing as nobody would tell me anything more than that.

I reached the ward, only to be faced with a whole corridor of closed doors. I asked a passing nurse which one I needed. She wasn't sure, but ran off to check. An orderly came back. "You want to see Tom Rivers?"

"Yes," I said.

"Follow me Miss...?"

"Rivers, Lucy Rivers. I'm his daughter."

"His wife is with him and the doctor, but I am sure they will be done in a moment," he said as he stopped outside a partially opened door. "I'll get you a seat so you can wait."

"Thank you."

I paced the corridor nervously, even though the orderly brought me a chair very quickly. Now that I was here, I had no idea what I was going to say, or how they would react to seeing me, and I prayed and prayed that Dad would be okay – and that the shock wouldn't give him another episode.

The doctor finally emerged, and I grabbed him before he could walk away on more of his rounds.

"Hi, um, I'm Lucy. Tom's daughter. I haven't seen him in over five years. I didn't leave under the best circumstances. I was a terrible daughter. But, I am just so worried about him, and I know now I love him so much and I was so stupid." I couldn't stop myself. The doctor looked mildly amused.

"Slow down. Your dad is doing fine. Now, I think you are asking me if I think seeing you might make your dad worse?" I gaped at him.

"How did you get that from all that?"

"I've been doing this job a long time. We learn how to interpret panic," he said soothingly. "Go on in. I'll bet he will be very happy to see you. And no, you won't do any damage to his heart. You may even help it heal up a bit quicker," he continued reassuringly.

I stood staring at the door.

"Go on in, Miss Rivers," he repeated, "don't make him wait any longer."

I took a deep breath, and opened the heavy door slowly.

I peeked in and saw my dad, lying there all hooked up to monitors and screens, things beeping all around. I wanted to cry, but managed to hold it together.

Steph looked up, and I tried to smile at her. It came out all wrong, and I just sobbed. I had expected her to be angry with me, to shout and yell, but she simply got up and just took me in her arms, no questions asked. I wrapped mine around her too and let her hold me while I cried. She let me go, and tenderly pushed my hair back behind my ears for me.

"Oh Lucy, it is so good to see you, sweetie," she breathed. "Your Dad and I have missed you so much." I squeezed her hand, unable to find any words at all to express how sorry I was for all that pain, but I think she knew anyway.

I moved over to the bed, and tucked my hand into my dad's. He opened his eyes, and I bent down to kiss him on his cheek. He tried to smile.

"Hey Dad, you just rest. We've got all the time in the world to talk once you're well again. I am so sorry. I love you so much." He closed his eyes again as a single tear rolled down his wrinkled cheek. He squeezed my hand real tight and I stayed by his side. Steph sat on the other side and we held hands over his lap. It was good to be back around family, even though my best friend, the man I had fallen head over heels for a second time, had turned out to be the sneakiest, most devious and horrible rat alive.

I would never forgive him for his betrayal. How could he do such a thing, to me and to Callie? She was such a lovely person, prepared to help him with his sister, and to even get her to give me a job? What kind of an asshole actually does that? Sadly, I knew that I would have to face him at some point, and knew he would be back here on Sunday with Morgan too. His time at the DA's office was now up. He had a week off before he began his new semester, and that meant he would be here, at home with his, our, family, especially given the circumstances. How on earth would I be able to face him, knowing what I now knew?

Steph and I drove home late that night. Dad had been doing well, responding to all the treatment he was being given. The attack had been a minor one, but it had been enough to shake us all up, that was for certain. We got into the house, and I noted the odd things here and there that she'd changed, but mainly it was still my old home.

"Thanks for not taking every bit of Mom out of here," I said to her.

She grinned.

"Lucy, your mom made this place so beautiful. I am not even close to being the designer she was, or from what I've heard, you are too. Cole told us all about your work and how well you are doing. We are so proud of you honey. Sounds like your first job is a doozy!"

"Thanks, I don't know how much of what Cole has told you is true, but despite everything I am glad he found me." There must have been a bit of an edge to my voice, and I should have remembered that Steph was the queen of picking up on the unspoken.

"What do you mean? I thought you and he were finally together?" Steph asked me gently. "We were so pleased for you both. He has loved you and only you his entire life, sweetie."

"He has a girlfriend already and I couldn't even hope to compete."

She shook her head in disbelief. "No. Cole and I talk

all the time Lucy. I am absolutely certain that if there was a girl who meant more to him than you do that I would have heard about it. The only other women in his life are Morgan, myself, and his best friend Callie."

"Yes, that's her. They were all over each other in the foyer of her company building. Kissing and cuddling, and in front of Morgan too!"

I had hoped to shock her, but clearly even my turning up out of the blue hadn't fazed her, and this wasn't likely to either so she just laughed at me.

"Oh Lucy, you have always been so impetuous, and so inclined to jump to conclusions. Callie has been Cole's best friend, along with Jacob, since they went to UCLA together. She and Jake are the couple – not her and Cole. I promise you."

I could hardly believe what I was hearing. But that still didn't excuse the fact he hadn't trusted me to make a go of my business alone, and had felt he needed to enlist his multi-millionaire friends to give me a job. I was a big girl. I didn't need some do-gooding, over-protective big brother. I needed a man who would love me, but let me make my own mistakes. One who would let me make it in my own way, and not interfere. And I would tell him so the very next time I saw him.

Steph laughed again. "That look is one I see constantly on Morgan's face. You two are so like your daddy. But that stubborn streak – you get all that from your mom, sweetheart! He'd do anything for you, you should know that by now. And none of us can do it alone," she said as if she had read my mind. "We all need a helping hand every now and again, and why shouldn't someone who worships the ground you walk on want to do whatever they can to help you succeed? And, I've met Callie. That girl doesn't do a thing she doesn't want to. She may well have agreed to meet with you, but I can bet you got that job on your own merits. She doesn't accept second best, ever."

13

COLE

Mom had warned me that Lucy was on the warpath.

I had no idea what I had done this time, but as I headed back to Newton with Morgan strapped securely in her car seat behind me I couldn't help but feel nervous. Lucy had always been a bit of a loose cannon, but Mom had said something about her getting her panties in a twist about Callie and me. I could have laughed as I thought of her and Jake waving us off this morning, their arms glued around one another, clearly enraptured. Still, I sang along with Morgan to her favorite nursery time songs CD, and prepared for the tongue-lashing I knew would be coming my way.

I had barely pulled up onto the driveway when Lucy emerged. Mom had quickly taken Morgan inside, as Lucy stormed toward me. "You are the biggest piece of shit on the planet," she yelled. "How could you? You cheating, lying sack of shit!"

"Okay, so I am a shit. We know this, always have, but

why specifically this time Lucy?" I asked, suddenly finding it all just too funny.

"You and Callie, and your mom tells me she is going steady with your friend too. How could you do that? Cheat on me, and go behind your best friend's back with his girlfriend? What kind of a monster are you? And getting me a job with her? How on earth were you ever going to manage to keep it all quiet, huh?"

I chuckled. I really shouldn't have. It was like a red cape to a bull. But the whole thing was so ludicrous.

"Lucy Rivers, you really are the most wonderful woman I have ever met. But you can also be the most ridiculously stupid. Callie is my best friend. Just like my mom told you. I have no idea what you think you may have seen or heard, but it is not what you think.

"Oh, I'm stupid now too?" she blurted and then poked a finger into my chest.

I frowned, thinking maybe I should wipe the smile off my face and take this seriously. "No, I didn't mean it like that..."

"Want a ladder for the hole you are digging, mister?"

I held up my hands trying to make her calm down. I needed to untie my tongue and explain.

"I dropped Morgan off at Glitch. Callie thanked me, yet again, for making her see just how much Jake adored her. They have been in cloud cuckoo land ever since I got them together at the Red Hot Chili Peppers gig. She helped me to take the photo of you so we were even. Then yes, I sent her your details. Getting you in for a meeting seemed like the least I could do to try and help you out considering how much I know I hurt you when I took my mom's side. But you, I promise you, did the rest.

Callie has not stopped raving about the absolute gem I have sent her. She said she was more than happy to take care of Morgan, it seemed more than a fair exchange for the favor I had done her in sending you her way."

Lucy looked at me, her cat-like eyes narrowed with skepticism. I wanted to pick her up and kiss every inch of her face, to make her see sense, until she knew just how much I adored her – but I knew that would be the worst thing I could do right now. I waited and let her think it all through. It seemed to take forever, and I began to agitatedly hop from one foot to the other.

"So, you weren't dating anyone else when we were talking by email and text?" she asked shrewdly.

Fuck, she had me there. Oh god this was going to sound so preposterous.

"Well, I was – but it really isn't what you think. You see, Jake entered an eating contest, and Callie bet me he wouldn't win and she forced me to sign up to 'Wooed and Won' and take out at least four girls." I gazed down at the gravel I was kicking about with my toe of my shoe. I knew it was true and it still didn't sound in any way plausible.

"That sounds like the lamest excuse I have ever heard, but at least there are people who would be able to corroborate your story."

I looked up at her, hearing a tone of mild amusement in her voice. She was grinning from ear to ear. "I called Callie this morning, after my chat with your mom last night. I wanted to be sure, but I couldn't resist getting you back just a tiny bit for not telling me who you were on 'Wooed and Won' right from the start. And since when are you hot enough to name yourself after a Greek god? Apollo, *really*?"

I stepped tentatively towards her. "So, you don't hate me then? You forgive me? Oh, please say you forgive me?" I begged.

"Well, you may have a lot of work to do to make it up to me, but I am sure we can think of something you can do that might get you back on my good side?"

"Would this help?" I asked as I took her into my arms. She melted into me ever so slightly.

"It might," she teased.

"How about this?" I brushed her lips tenderly with a kiss. I felt her shiver a little in my arms.

"Mmm, we may be getting somewhere."

"What about this?" I pressed my lips to hers, sliding my tongue gently across her bottom lip. She opened to me willingly, and I felt the gentle flickering of her tongue as it sought my own.

I dipped and tasted, she did the same. The kiss deepened and I felt her fingers running up the muscles of my back. I pulled her in as close to my body as I could, and lifted her so her feet were off the ground.

"I love you Lucy, I always have. I always will."

"I love you too," she breathed, her eyes welling up.

I took her chin, and held it lightly. "I know we are young, and I know people might think it's crazy, us being stepsister and stepbrother, but will you have me for the rest of my life? Will you marry me?" I murmured against her lips.

"What, you're not even going to get down on one knee?" she asked playfully.

"I will do whatever you want, my love. Your wish is my command!" I said as I dipped down, my knee touching the gravel.

She giggled and her eyes sparkled as I waited patiently for her answer.

"Get up you idiot," she said as she pulled back toward her body. "Oh yes, Mr. Kent, of course I will marry you. Now shut up and kiss me again."

She sighed as I dutifully obeyed, claiming her lips as my own from now until eternity. There was nothing I wouldn't do for Lucy Rivers, the woman that stole my heart all those years ago.

EPILOGUE - LUCY

I sat alone in the quiet room, staring at my reflection in the ornate mirror before me. My hands were steady, not even a hint of nerves, it was as if they knew I'd made the right decision.

Today was the day I'd let everything go from my past, no longer dwelling on it – moving on – and when I really thought about it, well, it was about time.

The corners of my lips flittered up into a smile as I considered the new beginning that awaited me, and with a final swipe of sparkling nude lipstick I was ready.

It was time.

"Are you done yet?" Alison's voice called through the door, frustrated that I hadn't let her in yet. "He's not going to wait forever you know... and neither can I!"

"Nonsense, he's waited how many years already? He can wait a few more minutes, it won't kill him. You take your time, hon!" said Callie, her voice muffled from also being locked out of my little sanctuary. "But you just let us know if you need any help."

It probably was time to let them in, I thought as I remembered the tiny pearl buttons that were just out of my reach, lined up in the middle of my shoulder blades.

But before I could open up and let my two bridesmaids in, a tiny rapping sounded at the door and a small but confident voice demanded entry. "Lucy, I have to show you my dress! Let me in!"

I imagined my new stepsister, Morgan, stomping her little foot, hands on her hips.

I drew in a breath, unlocked the door and took a step backward.

"Okay, you can come in now." I patted and smoothed at the lace material of the ivory dress as the door swung open.

Morgan was the first in and immediately came to stand before me, her head tilted up. "Well it's about time!" she said scolding me and I couldn't help but giggle at her frowning face.

I slipped my hand into Morgan's. "You look beautiful, just like Cinderella," she whispered.

"So do you, sweetie. Like a princess."

From the doorway I heard multiple gasps, Callie and Alison both stood with their hands covering their mouths, their eyes glossy.

"Oh my god, you look stunning, Luce!" Alison said as she enveloped me in a hug. A wayward tear escaped and streaked down Alison's face.

"Don't you dare start crying," I warned her. "You'll set me off, and I'll have to do my make-up all over again and then I really will be late!

"Absolutely breathtaking! Cole won't know what hit him," Callie said as she joined our little hugging session.

I stood like that for a few moments, holding on to each of them desperately beating back the threatening tears.

They'd all brought me so much joy and friendship over the last few months; I truly wondered how I'd ever gotten on without them. Especially Morgan, who was the most amazing little sister I could've ever asked for. I only hoped that one day that she would forgive me for not being a part of her life sooner; I'd missed so much of her growing up, I was determined to be there for her now and forever as a big sister should.

And then there was Callie, who was technically my boss, but we'd become increasingly close whilst working together. She was my inspiration, a savvy businesswoman with a heart of gold. Not to mention the most amazing singer! Cole and I had managed to twist her arm to be our singer for our first dance, and with her vocal range, she was the perfect person to perform Ella James' "At Last".

"Okay enough of all this soppy girly stuff, we don't want to crease your dress... plus you have somewhere you need to be!" Alison said as she quickly fastened the last few buttons of my dress. She was my rock. Being there for me when most friends would've discarded me without a second thought.

I nodded. "I'm ready," I said.

"God, you don't look nervous at all," Callie said. "I was a wreck when Jake proposed, so I'll probably be a ball of goo on our wedding day.

"There's nothing to be nervous of," I explained, "Cole's my soul mate. My one and only. I know without question he's the man I'm going to spend the rest of my life with... so why waste energy on nerves?"

"You said it, sister!" Alison chirped, whilst fluffing the edge of my dress.

"Come on," Morgan said impatiently, "Daddy's waiting."

"Okay, let's go," I replied ready to face my destiny, as Morgan led me out of the church's bridal dressing room, pulling as hard as she good. I think she was more excited than me to walk down the aisle. Alison and Callie followed dutifully behind.

※

My dad stood in his crisp grey suit, waiting patiently by the double doors to the main section of the church. His face transformed as Morgan and I turned the corner and he laid eyes on the both of us coming toward him.

"My girls," he whispered. He clasped a hand over his chest as if in pain, and a sudden worrying thought flashed across my mind. After his heart attack, he'd been ordered to take it easy and to adjust his diet to a healthier one, and he'd been doing really well – there hadn't been any repeat occurrence since.

He must've seen the concern on my face and shook his head. "No, sweetie, I'm fine. You look so beautiful, so much like your mother, it just makes my heart ache." He kissed me on the cheek and I took a tight hold of his arm.

A thick lump formed in my throat upon hearing of my mother, and I bit my tongue. I'd tried to go all morning without thinking about her absence, on how she should've been there with me; helping me with my make-up, fussing at my hair. But it was pointless to try and block her out. I knew at the very least, she was here in spirit.

My mom would be there when I walked down the aisle, she would be there when I give birth to her first grandchild; she'd always be by my side, deep within my heart. I'd never lock her out again.

Callie handed me a soft white handkerchief, and gratefully I took it, dabbing the corner of my eyes.

"Thanks," I whispered.

My mom would be proud I'd found a lasting happiness. And it was time to make my dreams, and hers, all come true.

The music from within the church changed, and the familiar Wedding March began. My dad led me to the side, away from the double wooden doors as they opened.

Callie knelt down and whispered in Morgan's ear, giving her a few words of encouragement, but that little girl, so stubborn and confident, knew exactly what she had to do. She grasped her little flower basket, filled with satin white petals, and with a last look to our father, she smiled and proceeded to march with a purpose down the aisle, scattering the fake flowers as she went.

A moment or so later, Callie winked at me and followed in Morgan's wake.

"Break a leg," Alison whispered as she disappeared through the doors.

It was our turn next, and I clamped my hand more securely around my dad's arm. A whole torrent of nerves decided now was the perfect time to swirl up a storm in my belly. I hadn't been lying before when I'd said I was cool as a cucumber at the thought of marrying my one true love, but now standing on the precipice of a life altering moment, I faltered.

We stood at the entrance as countless heads turned towards us. My eyes went as wide as they could; startled and afraid. All those people, friends and family, I thought, are watching me. What if I tripped over my dress and fell on my face?

A warm hand patted my own. "Don't look at them," my dad advised, "find Cole."

I understood. My eyes travelled all the way down the aisle before my feet ever did. I tried to ignore all the onlookers on the periphery, searching for the familiar figure at the end.

And then everything went silent. All the rustles and gasps from the guests were drowned out by the pure look of love in Cole's eyes.

Our eyes met, and nothing mattered anymore.

A calm came over me, as if Cole was wrapping me up into a protective blanket, shielding me from my own anxious thoughts.

And with his encouraging gaze, Cole slowly reeled me in and I found my feet moving on their own accord. I couldn't wait to reach him, to be by his side but I also never wanted the moment to end. With our eyes locked, our souls entwining, we were safe in our own bubble, where happiness reigned and sadness was denied entry.

But then I realized, every day would and could be like this. Staring into the eyes of the man I loved was all I ever wanted or needed.

My dad gently unwrapped himself from my grasp and led me the final steps towards Cole. I gasped at the sudden shock that he was right there before me already, his hand reaching for mine. The aisle had looked miles long a few seconds ago, as if it would've taken hours to reach him instead of mere moments.

"Wow," Cole breathed, his voice barely audible, as he threaded his fingers in-between mine. He guided me front and center, we were surrounded an all sides by the people we loved and who loved us. And for a second I thought I was dreaming, that it all couldn't possibly be real. But the feel of Cole at the ends of my fingertips told me I wasn't imagining things.

"Sorry I'm late." I blushed, as a spark of delight travelled up my arm from his gentle touch.

"I would wait an eternity for you," Cole whispered in reply. "I've always had faith that we'd get our second chance. And this time, I'm never ever going to let you go."

THE END

WANT MORE? READ AN EXCERPT FROM HOW TO LOVE A COWBOY

Pete

I closed the ledger and leaned back into the rich cherry colored leather of the desk chair. I closed my eyes and rubbed my temples, thinking about how much easier things had been when my father was around running things at Killarny Estate. It wasn't anything I hadn't become accustomed to over the years. Being the oldest of the five Killarny brothers, it was expected from birth that I would be the one to take over the day to day running of the ranch. While all the brothers were equal partners in running the ranch, it was I who was the most responsible. Ask anyone. It was also me that my dad had turned to back when my mother, Emily Killarny, had first been diagnosed with breast cancer.

At my mother's request, I took on the additional tasks that my father had usually taken care of. Most of it was business, the sort of thing that didn't capture my attention quite like the quiet, meditative work with the horses, but I knew what had to be done. Most of all, I hadn't wanted to let my mother down.

Emily Killarny was a force unto herself, but she had a kind and good heart, and above all, she loved her children. I was aware that I had a special place in her heart when she had gone out of her way to be the best kind of grandmother she could be to Emma. I'd been dejected and alone, raising a two year old daughter alone after my ex-wife, Kelly, decided one day that motherhood and married life wasn't for her. My parents had been so kind to us in the days following that abandonment, and I would forever be grateful to both of them. My mother had especially done all that she could to make sure that Emma felt safe and loved after her mother's abrupt departure.

Back then my major responsibilities had been tending to the horses, something I still loved and wished I was able to do more of, but being the oldest, and since my father had relocated to Costa Rica, I knew I had to be the one to step up to the plate. My mother's death three years prior had taken a toll on the family patriarch, and after suffering a severe bout of depression, he finally decided to make some major changes. One of those changes included leaving the states and relocating to a warmer climate, leaving the green Kentucky hills behind him in favor of sun and sand. Some days I couldn't help but feel a little jealous of that, but I knew that my heart would always be right here, wherever Emma was.

I opened my eyes again and looked at my computer screen for a moment before getting up and heading for the door, grabbing my jacket on the way. There was still a chill in the air that early in the Kentucky spring and it was invigorating to step out into the morning air, breathing in the fresh smell of new grass and the less pleasing scent wafting from the nearest barn. The smell of manure might not have appealed to everyone, but for me, it was a reminder of home and childhood.

I breathed in the air and made my way over to the stables where my brother Alex was brushing out the coat of a two year old mare.

"She looks beautiful," I said as I came up to stand on the other side of the stall door.

Alex nodded. "Siobhan is quite a looker." He brushed her russet coat to a glistening sheen that caught the early morning sun and made the horse look like a copper penny.

"You think we'll run her next year?" I asked him as I looked over the horse from nose to tail. She was beautiful, but I wasn't sure if she was one of the horses that we would end up taking to the many derbies we were involved in.

Alex shrugged. "Not sure. She hasn't been run that much, and I really think that if we had planned on doing that with her, she should have seen a little more practice at this point in her life. I think she is a great horse, but I'm not sure the derby life is the one for her. However, I do think she is going to give us a lot of talented foals."

Alex was probably the quietest of all the brothers, so hearing him talk this much was a little unusual. The only time Alex had much to say was when he was talking about a horse. Not much for words and usually keeping to himself, he was definitely the most horse whisperer like among us and was more involved with the training of individuals here at the ranch. He was so in tune with the horses that it helped to have his expertise around to help people become accustomed to green horses. While most of our horses were bred here on the ranch, we did keep a group of wild ponies from the Dakotas on one of the spreads of land that was fenced off from the rest. Alex's house was out there and visiting that part of the ranch felt like entering a wilderness. I could see why my parents had given him that parcel when they were divvying up the land to us. It fit my younger brother's personality perfectly, and he was never happier than he was when he was among the wild horses.

"Her mother is Spring, right?" I asked.

"Yeah, and her father was David's Lariat."

David's Lariat had been one of Alex's favorites. A horse that my father had acquired from a Colorado ranch when we were still very young, the horse had been a monster of an animal when we got him. He stood taller than any of our other horses but managed to be faster than almost any horse half his weight. He was a marvel and had produced many of our fastest horses. David's Lariat had died just a year before, but we still had a few of his offspring around the ranch and would likely see his influence in our derby horses for decades to come.

"Well, even if she isn't going to run for us, she's a beautiful girl, and I'm sure she'll give us a few great runners."

"What are you up to?" Alex asked as he put away the brush and stepped out of the stall to join me where I stood.

I shrugged. "Just needed to get out of the office for a little while."

"Already?" He looked at his watch. "It's early in the

day. Why don't you hire someone to take care of some of the stuff you don't enjoy? That's what bookkeepers are for, after all. It would give you a break and let you have a chance to get back out here with the horses where you want to be."

Alex was perceptive with more than just the horses.

"Yeah, well, I might do that after the next couple of derbies have passed. I've got too much on my plate right now to hand it over to someone totally new."

My brother sighed and shrugged. "Whatever you say. Just don't be afraid to ask for a little help when you need it."

I gave him a firm pat on the back and continued on down through the stables, past the stalls that housed our many horses. A few of our ranch hands were leading some of the horses out to graze in the pasture, while some of them were headed to the arena and our track for training. As I exited the other end of the massive stable, I saw Emma atop her horse, Saoirse.

"How'dya do, Miss Emma Lou?"

Emma frowned at me, and I could see her brow furrowing under her helmet. I knew she hated it when I referred to her middle name, Louise, but told myself that someday she would come to think of it as endearing, so I kept up the practice.

She tossed her head back. "Saoirse and I just went out for our morning run. I was about to take her back to the stable and then head in for my lessons. Is Hetty here yet?"

I shook my head. "She wasn't there when I left the house, but there's a good chance she's arrived by now. Better hurry on back, you don't want to be late."

My twelve year old daughter beamed at me from

where she sat on her horse and headed into the stable before dismounting. I watched her lead her young horse into the stall and couldn't help but notice how much she was starting to look like her mother. It wasn't a bad thing, but I did wonder how Emma would feel as she looked in the mirror and started to notice the resemblance she shared with the woman who left her—and me—behind when Emma was just a toddler.

I walked toward the pasture as I recalled the time directly after Kelly left. It had been a shock to me when it happened, but when I had a little time to think it over, nothing about it was too surprising. We had married straight out of high school, and my parents had been opposed to the match from the start. Kelly's parents were business owners in the nearest town, and ours had been the kind of wedding that made the local papers. Our courtship had been brief — we dated at the end of high school, and because I was an idiot, I had proposed to Kelly not long after graduation. We married and moved into a house here at Killarny Estate and had had a hell of a time for the first couple of years.

Kelly was wild and looking back I could tell she had been just a little too wild for me. It wasn't something I had noticed at the time, and while it was just the two of us, it was easy to forget that we were stepping into a new world that included all sorts of new responsibilities. Back then we would spend our weekends hopping around the bars in town before heading back to the privacy of our house at the ranch and going at it like rabbits. It was no surprise when Kelly got pregnant, and I was overjoyed, but she didn't seem too enthused about it. Slowly she warmed to the idea, and once Emma was born, I could see that she really did love our daughter.

Things were never the same though. Kelly never looked at me the same way, and I tried to encourage her to go see a doctor to see if what she was struggling with was postpartum depression, but she wouldn't listen.

I came home one evening to find all of Kelly's things gone, a note on the kitchen table, and Emma wailing in her playpen. I had picked up my daughter and the note and read the words through tears as Emma sniffled and buried her head against my shoulder. Kelly was gone. She apologized in the letter, said she was heading to California to pursue her dream of being an actress, and that she was going with her friend, Bud.

Bud was the guy she had dated before me in high school, and suddenly it all started to make sense. We never really heard from her after that, aside from a Christmas card or a birthday present for Emma on the years that Kelly remembered, which were few and far between.

As far as I knew, Emma had no real memory of her mother. It made me sad, but I wondered if it was for the best that she didn't know what she was missing out on. If Kelly had hung around much longer, it would have been more difficult than it already was to get Emma used to not having her mother around.

I had been so grateful to my parents for the support they were during that time, especially my mother. She had done all she could to be the maternal figure in my daughter's life, but she never stopped pressing me to go on dates and get out there again, constantly reminding me that I was still young and there was happiness out there for me if I would just go looking for it.

Her last attempt had been just a few years before she passed away when I had first hired Hetty Blackburn, a local teacher, to be Emma's tutor. The ranch was well out of the way, and it was quite a hike to the nearest school, so I had decided to homeschool Emma. It gave her a chance to be around the horses more and to study at her own pace, which was quite a bit faster than the average elementary school student, according to Hetty.

Hetty was pretty and a very sweet woman. Her black hair and blue eyes were a sort of bewitching combination that was hard to ignore, but I couldn't get back into dating; not then and not now, even though it was 10 years since Kelly walked out. Even if I hadn't already been very hesitant to date, Hetty already had one major strike against her—she knew my daughter.

I leaned against the bright white fence and watched as a group of our horses played together in the dewy field that was filled with clover. The place was even more picturesque than usual in this light. Killarny Estate was really something to be proud of, and I was so glad to have the privilege of being a part of a four generation horse ranch, the largest one in Kentucky, and now, for all intents and purposes, running the place.

One rule I had established for myself was that until I knew I could trust a woman, she would never meet my daughter. And since I wasn't in the mood to start dating yet, nothing had ever made it that far. Sure, I had been with women since Kelly—too many to count—but I was there to get what I wanted and get out. I never went out with anyone that I thought was there for more than what

I was because I had more heart than that. But I didn't trust anyone to give me any more than what I was looking for at the moment. It was sex, pure and simple—though rarely pure or simple. I was there for a release, to have sex, hear them scream my name, and then leave quietly. The closest I had ever come to bringing a woman home was the Lawrence girl who I made it all the way back to the ranch with, but we never left my truck. We had made it as far as the pecan grove when I pulled over and had her right there in the cab of my pickup. When we were done, I turned around and drove her right back to her house. But that had been the last one, and that had been a long time ago now.

There was no need to complicate my life any more than it already was and I was certainly not going to bring any of these women into the life of my daughter. She had already experienced enough pain from my poor choices, and I wasn't going to do that to her again.

My middle brother, Jake, came riding up on his stallion and brought the horse to a quick halt a few feet away from me.

"Showing off?" I asked as I cocked my eyebrow at him.

He swung down off the saddle and gave the horse a pat. "This bastard is ready to run!"

Clement certainly looked like he was ready for it. His eyes were wild, but it was clear that he was happy after his morning run with Jake.

"Think about how fast he's going to be with one of the jockeys on him!"

I nodded. "We're taking him to the Waters derby, right?"

"Yup, just a couple of weeks away now."

I noted to myself that I needed to check that out on the calendar. There was still a lot left to do in preparation, and we weren't sure how many horses we would be taking. Clement was certainly on the top of the list, but I knew we needed to have a few backups. Killarny Estate had always been top of the pack as far as producing some of the fastest race horses in the country, but ever since my father had packed it up and gone to Costa Rica, it felt like we had lost some of our edge. I had no idea what it was Dad had that we didn't quite have down yet, other than the forty years of experience. What I did know was that it was crucial for us to win this derby. Things were tight, and if we were going to turn them around and maintain things the way they were around here, or if we were ever going to have any hope of making Killarny the very best again, we had to win the Waters derby.

"You coming?" Jake asked me as he brushed his reddish-brown hair back out of his face and wiped his brow with the back of his sleeve.

I looked at him bewildered. "Of course I am."

He shrugged. "Don't act like it's a given. You haven't been there in years."

"Yeah, well...now I don't really have any choice, do I? Dad is still in Costa Rica, and I don't know the next time he's planning on coming back, so I've got to be there to represent the ranch. And I think Emma would enjoy the trip to Tennessee, so yeah, I'll be there."

"You're not nervous, are you?" Jake winked at me, and I frowned in response.

"Why would I be nervous?"

"Because," he began, pausing to spit on the ground.

"Little Sara Waters is going to be there. I wonder if she is going to follow you around like she always used to when we were kids."

I rolled my eyes. "Sara Waters is thirty by now. I am sure she has got better things to do than chase around a nearly middle-aged man with his twelve year old daughter in tow."

"Hey now, don't write yourself off just yet. You're only a year or so older than her, right? I bet she would be champing at the bit to get a piece of a Killarny brother."

I shook my head and started off back toward the stable, Jake following behind me with Clement.

"Then she can have her pick of the other four. Hell, she can have both Stephen and Sam if she wants them." I stopped and looked around. "Speaking of that, where are the twins?"

Jake shrugged as he continued toward the stable. "Who the hell knows. They're out every night of the week. Probably still in bed."

I knew he was kidding about the last thing. If we had been taught anything as kids, it was that getting up early in the morning was the Killarny way.

"Okay, well. I need to go find them. I'll get back to you about the Waters derby. We need to talk about some logistics getting there, but it can wait until later."

As I walked off toward the other barns to locate my two youngest brothers, I couldn't help thinking about what Jake had said regarding Sara Waters. I hadn't seen her since we were practically teenagers. It must have been a decade or so. I wondered what she looked like now and if there was a chance that we'd get some time alone when I was at her father's derby in a few weeks.

GET A FREE BOOK!

Join my mailing list to be the first to know of new releases, free books, special prices and other author giveaways.

http://freehotcontemporary.com

ALSO BY JESSA JAMES

Bad Boy Billionaires

Lip Service

Rock Me

Lumber Jacked

Baby Daddy

Billionaire Box Set 1-4

The Virgin Pact

The Teacher and the Virgin

His Virgin Nanny

His Dirty Virgin

Club V

Unravel

Undone

Uncover

Cowboy Romance

How To Love A Cowboy

How To Hold A Cowboy

Beg Me

Valentine Ever After

Covet/Crave

Kiss Me Again

Handy

Bad Behavior

Bad Reputation

ABOUT THE AUTHOR

Jessa James grew up on the East Coast but always suffered a severe case of wanderlust. She's lived in six states, had a variety of jobs and always comes back to her first true love – writing. Jessa works full time as a writer, eats too much dark chocolate, has an iced-coffee and Cheetos addiction, and can't get enough of sexy alpha males who know exactly what they want – and aren't afraid to say it. Dominant, alpha-male insta-luv is her favorite to read (and write).

Sign up HERE for Jessa's Newsletter:

http://jessajamesauthor.com/mailing-list/

Follow me on BookBub:

www.ingramcontent.com/pod-product-compliance
Lightning Source LLC
LaVergne TN
LVHW011836060526
838200LV00053B/4065